Sweetie

Sweetie

KEVIN O CONNOR

Published by K.O. Publications Ltd.,
7 Herbert Street, Dublin 2, Ireland.

ISBN
0 9536302 0 X (HARDBACK)
0 9536302 1 8 (PAPERBACK)

Printed & Bound in Dublin, by Betaprint Ireland.
Layout & Design, CSet & Design, Dublin • Felix McGinley.

Prints: © Anne Woodfull Saunders.

CONTENTS

FOREWORD

I would like to acknowledge the contributions of many who helped to make this difficult adventure possible.

Firstly, there was my chief researcher, colleague BRENDAN KEENAN, who is the Group Finance Editor of Independent Newspapers. His carefully prepared research and invaluable advice ensured the eventual launch of SWEETIE.

Editor, MICHAEL P. O'KANE, journalist and barrister, had a difficult job to do, but he did it with dedication, professionalism and immense patience.

PATRICK BOLAND, who produced the highly successful "Tales from a City Farmyard", helped me to blaze the do-it-yourself publishing trail, with his invaluable expertise in this area.

DONIE BOLGER, a superb strategist, was in charge of the serial rights negotiations and was an invaluable help with his practical wisdom.

And last and never forgotten was my partner, ANNE, who completed the sketches for this book. She assisted also with the research and was an inspiration to me – as all the team was – in overcoming the many difficulties.

The project, of course, could never have materialised without the most important people of all – my contacts in the security and political arena who, gave me excellent information, often at considerable risk to their own position and reputation.

1

GOLFING TRIP
TO ORLANDO

A party of golfers was preparing for a "trip of a lifetime" at Dublin Airport. They were the guests of millionaire businessman Ben Dunne and they were on their way to play the courses on the 1,500 acre Grand Cypress Resort in Mid Florida, near the world renowned Disneyworld in Orlando.

The nine-hour trip with a one-hour stop in Gander, Newfoundland, was uneventful, remembered only for the banter and good humour of the Irish contingent. After a rigorous security check at the airport, the party which included former Galway Mayor John Mulholland, Galway businessman Mick Heaslip and his solicitor Noel Smyth were chauffeured to their destination just 18 miles from the Airport and 20 miles from downtown Orlando.

This award-winning resort is designed around a tropical water-splashed setting near Sea World, Universal Studios and Walt Disney's Magic Kingdom, the Epcot Centre and the MGM theme park.

One of the main reasons for the visit was to test the calibre of the Grand Cypress Golf Club. In the privacy and calmness of the Jack Nicklaus-designed club, they demonstrated their golfing skills and the Irish capacity for good fun. Surrounded by unspoiled natural beauty, the North, South and East courses of the Grand Cypress provided an exceptional challenge for the Irish golfers, many of whom are low handicappers. Their favourite was the New Course modelled on the world famous

Old Course at St. Andrews which has cherished memories for Jack Nicklaus.

Most of the party had returned to Ireland when they read about Ben Dunne's "problems" in the Irish Sunday papers. Luckily for Dunne, his solicitor did not leave with the others, for when things went disastrously wrong, the lawyer gave his troubled host a lot of support.

2

SWANSONG OF
A TAOISEACH

It had been a traumatic, tear-filled week for Charles J. Haughey. On Tuesday morning, February 11th, 1992, he was still Taoiseach and the most powerful man in the country. A couple of hours later, he was a mere backbencher, adrift, like most of his former cabinet colleagues, stripped of his title, his power and literally his office. The pint-sized premier had arrived punctually at 9.30 a.m. at his showcase Merrion Street Office, with its adjoining dining room, sitting room, bathroom and kitchen. An hour later, in the Dáil chamber he formally announced his resignation as leader of the Government. He talked of the "deep affection for this House and its traditions" which he had developed over his 35 years as a T.D.

In the VIP section of the Dáil gallery overhead, tears glistened on the cheeks of his loving daughter, Eimear, as she listened to her father's farewell speech. Like her brother, Conor, she was particularly touched to hear him quote from Shakespeare's Julius Caesar: *"When beggars die there are no comets seen. The heavens will blaze forth the death of princes"*. Passing on the baton to his successor, Albert Reynolds, Charles Haughey quoted from Othello:
"I have done the state some service; they know it.
No more of that."
If he appeared measured and controlled in the Dáil chamber on Tuesday, it was because he was emotionally spent. It was particularly touching to see all his old colleagues from every

party wish him "bon voyage". A week of departing from the uppermost echelons of politics had proved to be interminable.

A fortnight previously, he announced his "lonely decision" to the Fianna Fáil parliamentary party in the big room on the fifth floor of Leinster House. The following night, shortly after 9 o'clock, when celebrations for his son Ciaran's wedding were getting into full swing at his magnificent mansion at Abbeyville, Kinsealy, on the north side of Dublin, a couple of the guests became tearful at the prospect of the Taoiseach's retirement. He turned to them and chided: "Don't be sad. I'm not. I'm relieved". A week before he retired, schoolchildren had been calling to the gates of Government Buildings with bunches of daffodils. Inside, the secretarial staff made small bundles of St. Christopher medals arriving for the Boss from all over the country. Every message and letter was left on the Taoiseach's desk "so that he would know how much he'll be missed", explained a member of his staff later. She added: "It's been incredible. Every single senior civil servant wrote him a personal letter saying goodbye. As far as I know, that is unprecedented."

There were messages from world leaders. They included: George Bush, Brian Mulrooney, Bob Hawke *("there is life after politics")*; Senator Edward Kennedy and the 72-year-old Italian prime minister, Giulio Andreotti, who once made the famous remark: "Power ruins whoever does not possess it".

Monday, the 10th of February was one of the hardest days of all for C.J. Haughey. There were presentations by his private staff. They included: Donagh Morgan, his private secretary; special advisor Eileen Foy; his personal secretary, Catherine Butler; Northern Ireland advisor Dr. Martin Mansergh; and Arts advisor Tony Cronin. According to his staff, they powdered him up and dried his eyes for his meeting with SDLP leader John Hume, winner of the Nobel Peace prize in October 1998.

Hume, who became leader of the SDLP a month before Charles Haughey won the Fianna Fáil race in December, 1979, called to thank him on behalf of the party "for everything he had done to keep Northern Ireland high on the political agenda". He also thanked him for the courtesy and openness he had always shown himself and he said that a lot of people in Northern

Ireland had talked to him about "how they would miss Mr. Haughey". After an emotional John Hume left, Peter Cassells, general secretary of the Irish Congress of Trade Unions and a key negotiator in the Government-union talks, called to the Taoiseach's office to bid him farewell on behalf of the country's trade unions.

Next it was the turn of the entire Department of the Taoiseach to say their goodbyes. Among the 200 or so who filled the conference room of the second floor of Government Buildings were the then Attorney General, Harry Whelehan, the Secretary to the Government, Dermot Nally, the Secretary to the Department of the Taoiseach, Padraig O hUiginn, the staff from Abbeyville and the Taoiseach's wife, Maureen Haughey, who was visibly moved by the emotion in the room. The staff presented their departing Boss with first edition (1791) Volumes I and II of Grosses Antiquities of Ireland. Mrs. Haughey was presented with an 18-carat gold Celtic brooch - a replica of one of the treasures in the National Museum - and a bouquet of her favourite flowers, lilies.

There were cheers and tears as Dermot Nally recalled his first encounter with Charles Haughey 35 years ago when they worked together on a report for the Seanad. The Taoiseach at that time was Mr. Haughey's father-in-law, Sean Lemass, one of Ireland's outstanding leaders. Mr. Haughey paused several times in his speech of reply.

And while a "tearful" Padraig O hUiginn escorted Mrs. Haughey back to her car, the cleaning staff of the Taoiseach's department – who had waited two hours for their turn – presented Mr. Haughey with a Mass bouquet. That was followed by a special moment for Mr. Haughey's official drivers, Max Webster and Bobby O'Brien. After nearly a half-century between them of driving the Boss around the country, they posed for their first and last photograph with him in the office of the Taoiseach. The Boss had been particularly generous with the two policemen. He changed the retirement age of the Gardaí - to ensure a couple of years extra work for his drivers. And he also looked after their families when jobs were needed. While working for CJ, because of the guaranteed overtime, they were among the highest paid policemen in the force. When Max Webster and his wife celebrated their 25th wedding anniversary, Haughey had a special present for them. He handed Max an envelope and inside were two tickets to New York, two train tickets from New York to Los Angeles and two return tickets by air from Los Angeles to Dublin.

At 2 o'clock on Monday, the 10th of February, the Taoiseach travelled the short distance over to Fianna Fáil headquarters in Mount Street for yet another farewell party hosted by the general secretary Pat Farrell and the 13 staff. They presented him with a silver salver from the Armada collection, made by Sleaters Jewellers in Johnson's Court. Standing under the imposing portrait of Eamon de Valera, the founder of Fianna Fáil who gave 35 years' service to the nation as Taoiseach and President, Mr. Haughey spoke of the "momentous decisions" that had been taken there over the years. He recalled having been in that room with all three of Fianna Fáil's previous leaders, Eamon de Valera, Sean Lemass and Jack Lynch. And he mentioned the "frenzy" that filled the room during general election counts when he used to leave Mount Street for the RTE studios to accept either victory or defeat during his 12 years at the helm.

After a meeting with the new Taoiseach, Albert Reynolds, back in his office on Monday afternoon to discuss the hand-over of Government leadership, Charles Haughey made the journey to Aras an Uachtarain at 5 p.m. to inform President Mary Robinson that he intended to formally announce his retirement from the office of the Taoiseach in Dáil Eireann the following day.

On Monday night, twenty of his closest advisors, friends and family, including his loyal media "guru" P.J. Mara, his devoted and courteous private secretary Catherine Butler, his solicitor and long time friend Pat O'Connor, and his political buddy Brian Lenihan, gathered at his Abbeyville mansion for a private drinks' party. The Cabinet had already presented him with a piece of George 111 silver, organised by Ray Burke, Mary O'Rourke and Gerry Collins.

By Tuesday, the 12th of February his office in Government buildings had been cleared of all his effects, including his two favourite paintings, Paul Henry's 'Connemara' and Nathaniel Hone's 'St. Doughlac's Church'.

His children, Eimear, Conor and Sean (Ciaran was still on his three-week honeymoon in Singapore) were already in the Public Gallery when he entered the chamber. Maureen Haughey had decided not to attend on the grounds that it was a day for the Reynolds family. But Mrs. Haughey joined her husband, her children, son-in-law John Mulhearn, daughters-in-law, and Government press secretary P.J. Mara for lunch in the private dining room of Mr. Haughey's favourite haunt, Le Coq Hardi ... a restaurant with cherished and abiding memories for Mr. Haughey.

Afterwards, Mr. Haughey returned to his office in Government Buildings. And shortly before the Dáil resumed at 3.30 p.m., he left for the last time as Taoiseach. As he walked through the glass tunnel connecting Government buildings to Leinster House, seven Gardaí and five uniformed ushers stood in line to salute him.

Sitting in the back of the chamber he listened as Albert Reynolds read out the names of the new Cabinet. He was surprised to learn that eight of his former Cabinet had been dropped from the line-up.

When he left the chamber at 6.30 p.m., Charles Haughey had no office. Accompanied by P.J. Mara, Catherine Butler and Donagh Morgan, he took the lift to the fourth floor and Brian Lenihan's office. It was poignant and ironic. After all their years as numbers one and two in the government, here were the newly retired Taoiseach and the Tanaiste he had sacked more than a year previously, talking nostalgically about old times.

Mr. Haughey was looking forward to his retirement ... and the quality years, not realising that a drama was about to unfold 3,000 miles away that would have powerful repercussions for himself, for his family, his friends, and indeed for the whole country.

3

HIGH DRAMA ON
THE 17th FLOOR

It was a typically clear morning in March in tropical Florida when Sheriff's deputy Ed Wright was cruising in his police car. An attempted suicide call broke the silence at exactly 9.13 a.m. on Thursday, March 20th, 1992. The call came from the Hyatt Regency Grand Cypress Hotel, a 1,500-acre resort just 18 miles from Orlando Airport and within two miles of the Disneyworld complex. Nearby, Chicago-born deputy Stan Spanich had finished his coffee break and just climbed into his police car when he also heard the call. Stan had been working the area around Disneyworld.

Nine minutes later, the two officers arrived almost simultaneously at the Hyatt Regency Grand Cypress, one of the premier holiday resorts in Florida. As the immaculately dressed bell boys with their colonial-type white helmets and white uniforms opened the glass doors, a lady executive, distressed and very excited, shouted that somebody on the seventeenth floor was attempting suicide. The officers ignored the crowds in the lobby, a dome-shaped plaza from which all the main corridors lead back into the main hotel. And they took no notice of a white-haired budgie, facing the spacious doors. He seemed to know something, for he kept squawking at the puzzled guests: "Well done! Well done!"

The police officers jumped on the elevator. As they raced from the lift, they saw on the corridor the tall figure of a big man, hands in the air in a v-shape as if about to dive into the gathering crowd underneath. He was screaming and calling for the police. At the same time, he was shouting to the two officers: "Get away! Get away!"

Spanich, an experienced counsellor, began to talk to him. "What's the problem? Are you ok?"

Screaming to the officers, the agitated man shouted: "I am surrounded; keep them away." He was getting closer to the railings, his hands still in the air.

Deputy Stan tried to re-assure him and win his confidence. He spoke in a soft voice: "Are you o.k; what's the matter; what's going on? I am the police."

At this stage, Officer Wright deliberately hid in a passageway so that he could not be seen from the balcony.

Deputy Stan slowly edged his way forward, closing the fifteen-foot gap between them.

The man seemed to panic and shouted at him: "I am going to take you with me." He was foaming at the mouth and his eyes were rolling.

Deputy Stan also panicked a little. He shouted: "I have a young family; I don't want to get hurt; I don't want to get hurt."

At this stage, the officer adopted a crouched position – a technique to try to re-assure the victim. The objective was to coax the victim into the crouched position.

Stan asked what was his name. In a soft voice, the big man replied: "Ben."

The officer volunteered "I am Stan."

A bit calmer now, the man said: "I go by my first name." He casually mentioned that he was in the textile business. Deputy Stan responded: "That must be interesting."

Spanich asked him if he was married. He said he was.

Again attempting to assuage his fears and win his confidence, Deputy Stan told him he had two girls, nine and eight, and a six-year-old boy.

Ben responded that he had a couple of kids too.

Stan assured him that he did not want anything to happen to him.

Desperately trying to get his mind off his suicide mission, Deputy Stan asked him the ages of his children. Later he casually asked him if he wanted a drink.

The Deputy did not know that the big Irishman he was trying to coax down from the balcony was one of Ireland's top businessmen, supermarket boss Ben Dunne. He had no way of knowing, either, that Dunne had gone through a horrendous experience in 1981 when he was kidnapped by the IRA and held prisoner for a full week, before he eventually escaped in the middle of the night by jumping into an open grave in a cemetery along the border with Northern Ireland. He had been held for seven days with a hood over his head and said later that he felt like "a caged animal" in constant fear of being shot.

Now, high up in a Florida tower and in a distressed state, he was reliving his kidnap nightmare. He screamed: "They are going to hurt me."

Deputy Stan re-assured him: "No one is going to hurt you."

They were talking for about 40 minutes when Stan suggested that they should go back to his room where they could "relax a little bit".

Still agitated and foaming at the mouth, Ben repeated: "They are going to hurt me."

In a determined voice, Stan responded: "I will guarantee you, I will be with you until this is all over." As he said it, Stan raised his hand as if swearing.

That seemed to strike a re-assuring chord with the big Irishman. Ben, now less agitated, responded: "If I get out of this, I will take care of you. If you guarantee me safety out of the country, I will take care of you." Dunne then offered the police officer some money.

Stan, figuring the guy was just blowing off steam, immediately responded: "That is not necessary. That is my job."

Officer Stan was beside Ben Dunne and began to walk towards his room. As they entered the hallway, Officer Wright and another Detective who had been lying in hiding nearby waiting for an opportunity to intervene, jumped on him and handcuffed him.

Stan kept re-assuring him: "They are not going to hurt you."

The detectives searched for ID. In the right front pocket of his trousers a zip locked-bag containing a white substance was found. It turned out to be cocaine.

Detective Chris Ford who arrived at the Grand Cypress just

21

after his uniformed colleagues Wright and Spanich, interviewed a witness, Ms. Denise Marie Wojcik. She said she was a prostitute hired by Dunne. She said that she and an associate, Sherri, arrived at the resort around 10 p.m. the previous night. Wojcik, who said she worked for an agency "Escorts in a Flash", went to Dunne's suite. In his statement later, Detective Ford said that Wojcik told him that Dunne had ripped her off (failed to pay for services provided). Wojcik later retracted this and said that Dunne did not rip her off. She told them she had seen Mr. Dunne using a large quantity of cocaine. A rescue squad was called and she was taken to Sand Lake Hospital where she was treated and released.

In an interview later with the "Sun" newspaper, Wojcik revealed how she and Ben Dunne snorted cocaine. In her lurid account, she described how they had taken part in a seven hour cocaine-sniffing session, sprinkling lines of the drug on to the rim of the sunken jacuzzi and inhaling it through rolled up $100 bills. But Mr. Dunne began acting strangely, she said, when he couldn't open the bedroom safe. She said that they discussed sex, but she told Dunne that none of the girls in her agency had sex with a client.

After interviewing Ms. Wojcik, Detective Ford stated that he searched Mr. Dunne's room. In a small black suitcase on the floor of the foyer of No 1708 he found several credit cards in Dunne's name, travel documents showing Mr. Dunne had booked nine rooms for associates, and a plastic bag containing 32.5g of cocaine. There was white powder at three locations in the suite together with rolled up bank notes apparently used to snort cocaine. The safe was opened by hotel staff and found to contain $9,738 in cash and £4,000 Irish. The cash, the black suitcase with its contents – a cocaine-dusted Bank of Ireland access card and Mr. Dunne's cocaine-covered membership card for the plush Michael Smurfit owned K Club in County Kildare – were all taken away as evidence by the police.

The big Irishman was put on a stretcher and also taken to Sand Lake Hospital by ambulance for possible cocaine overdose. Officers Wright and Stanich accompanied him. At the hospital, Ben lost control again. Reliving his IRA nightmare, he shouted, with his hands in the air: "They are going to hurt me." A Doctor came with a stethoscope. Ben reacted badly. He still had that frightened look in his eyes and refused to let anyone touch him until Stan said: "It is going to be okay. I will be here with you all the time." He was treated and cleared medically. A few minutes later, the officers started to walk him towards the police car. Ben shouted again: "They are going to hurt me". He began struggling and was handcuffed and shackled in what the police called a "hog-tie position" – handcuffs and feetcuffs joined together with a nylon tie. The officers had to forcibly push him inside the police car. Deputy Stan sat beside him and constantly tried to re-assure him as they drove to the Orange County jail police station, where Ben was charged.

Almost three months later to the day when the millionaire Irish businessman was found dishevelled and distressed on the 17th floor landing of the Hyatt Regency Grand Cypress Hotel, his case came up at Orange County Circuit Court. It was dealt with in just over ten minutes. In an unusual concession, the court permitted Mr. Dunne to speak by telephone from Dublin and plead his defence. His American lawyer, Butch Slaughter, was with him. A charge of trafficking cocaine was dropped after his defence successfully argued that the search of the room at the hotel was illegal. The court decided that he would have to undergo a 28-day drugs treatment course in the Charter Clinic in Chelsea, London, and pay a $5,000 fine together with State costs of $700. There were other stipulations. He was required to be available for at least 12 months for aftercare that involved regular monitoring of his condition. That was to be organised by his Dublin lawyer, Noel Smyth. He was also to abstain from alcohol for a year. If Mr. Dunne failed to comply with the court's rulings, he would be banned permanently from entering the United States. At the court hearing, his US visa was withdrawn.

But the court sanctions from this wild escapade were minuscule compared to the pending fall-out on his business empire and the effect that was to have not only on his own future within the huge family business, but also upon friends to whom he had been more than generous with company funds. And the man who was to suffer most of all was former Taoiseach, Charles Haughey, whom he had rescued from dire financial straits with huge donations of cash.

4

HAUGHEY LOSES
LUST FOR POWER

After all the years of wheeling and dealing and phone calls in the middle of the night to garner support and bully his detractors, why did Charles Haughey give up the ghost so easily? It was not one single thing, but a combination of reasons that forced him to timidly vacate his hallowed position in the end. For a number of years, Haughey was concerned that his former Minister for Justice, Sean Doherty, would disclose Cabinet details of the tapping of journalists phones in the Haughey-led government of 1982. Doherty had been hinting that he was prepared to "blow the lid" on the whole affair. CJ's loyal lieutenant and deputy leader, the late Brian Lenihan, was dispatched to Roscommon to try to persuade him to keep quiet. Lenihan had a special rendezvous with Doherty on his boat in Carrick-on-Shannon. Over drinks and coffee, they spoke for a couple of hours. But the mission was unsuccessful. Doherty, at that time, was in the parliamentary wilderness, having been forced to resign from the party over a phone-tapping affair. He bluntly told Lenihan that he was ready to "lift the lid" on what happened in 1982 unless he was immediately re-instated into the Fianna Fáil party.

Haughey was preparing for a trip to Libya to meet Col Gadaffi. He told Lenihan to call a meeting of the parliamentary party and re-instate Doherty during his absence. In that way, Haughey could distance himself from the whole affair. Doherty was re-instated at that party meeting. And though he huffed and puffed, he kept quiet about the 1982 government. Then for some unknown reason and a full ten years after the event, he called a press conference in the Montrose Hotel on Tuesday, 21st of January 1992 and in a bombshell announcement, revealed damaging details of Haughey's involvement in the tapping of journalists' phones during the lifetime of his minority government of 1982.

In a tense-filled voice in a special room in the Montrose Hotel, on the south side of Dublin, Sean Doherty, then Cathaoirleach of the Seanad, the fourth most powerful person in the country, read from a prepared statement, with his wife Maura sitting beside him. She was there to continue reading the statement in the event of Doherty breaking down.

His opening paragraph said it all. It read: "I am confirming that the Taoiseach, Mr. Haughey, was fully aware in 1982 that two journalists' phones were being tapped and that he at no stage expressed a reservation about this action." He gave damaging details on the problems confronting the crisis-riddled Haughey-led Government at that period. He said that between March and November of 1982 there were a number of serious leaks from the Cabinet that generated considerable concern within Government. It was his function as Minister for Justice to take steps to prevent such leaks.He sought the advice of Deputy Garda Commissioner Joe Ainsworth who was Head of Security and he recommended the option of tapping the phones of *Irish Independent* political journalist Bruce Arnold and of Geraldine Kennedy, later to become the political correspondent of the *Irish Times*.

He added: "As soon as the transcripts from the taps became available, I took them personally to Mr. Haughey in his office and left them in his possession." Anticipating a quick Haughey denial, he went into more detail: "I understand that the Taoiseach has already denied that this happened, so I wish to reiterate it in specific terms. Mr. Ainsworth forwarded to me the transcripts relevant to the Cabinet leak problem. Each and every one of those relevant transcripts were transported by me to Mr. Haughey's office and handed to him directly. He retained all but one of them, making no comment on their content. At no stage did he indicate disapproval of the action which had been taken."

Haughey followed the dramatic Doherty revelations the next day by a brilliant rebuttal at a hurriedly called news conference.

The problem with the Haughey performance was that no one believed him! He categorically denied what Senator Doherty had said and strongly refuted allegations that he had seen or been given transcripts of the taps by the former Minister for Justice. The Taoiseach's statement read: "I wish to state categorically that I was not aware at the time of the tapping of these telephones and that I was not given and did not see any transcripts of the conversations. I also wish to say that I have always abhorred the principle of phone-tapping, except where absolutely necessary to prevent serious crime or subversion by paramilitary organisations."

5

THE
ROSCOMMON
GARDA AFFAIR

I recall that Haughey-led Government of 1982 vividly, and particularly the part played in it by the Justice Minister Sean Doherty from County Roscommon. I have good reason to remember the whole affair in great detail, for I got involved in digging for a story about Doherty in his home constituency, and earned myself a three-week suspension from the *Sunday Independent* for my trouble!

The saga began when I got a tip off from a senior Garda source that strange goings-on in Sean Doherty's home county of Roscommon were worth investigation. I was told to talk to the Gardaí in the region - in particular Sergeant Tom Tully of Boyle, right in the heart of Doherty's home patch.

In his bungalow home on the outskirts of the town, Tully, a quiet-spoken officer, described political interference from Doherty as "unbearable" and told me about the Minister's attempt to transfer him - for doing his job. The transfer failed because of prompt intervention by the then deputy Garda Commissioner at the time, Larry Wren. At a special hearing to decide on whether Tully should be moved, Wren voted with the Garda Sergeants and Inspectors organisation representative, Derek Nally, against the proposal. Doherty later berated Wren for voting as he did. Tully's detailed story was followed by similar tales from five other gardaí who gave me signed statements about the extent of Doherty's interference. Apparently the Minister for Justice was doing everything but administering justice.

I returned to Dublin and asked to speak to former Tanaiste, the late George Colley. I met him in his Leinster House office. When I entered, he locked both doors and took the two telephones off the hook. He amplified certain points in the story and pleaded with me to give him a copy of the signed garda statements for a specially called meeting of the Fianna Fáil parliamentary party the next day. Kildare deputy, Charlie McCreevy (later to be a Minister for Finance) had put down a motion of no confidence in Charlie Haughey. "This could be dynamite at the meeting," Colley said to me. I refused the request because I did not want to get embroiled in internal Fianna Fáil problems. Anyway, I said, the *Sunday Independent* would be publishing the story the following Sunday. On Wednesday, October 13th, 1982, twenty-two Fianna Fáil deputies, including George Colley and Ministers Des O'Malley and Dr. Martin O'Donoghue, voted no confidence in Charles Haughey. But he still won by a sizeable majority.

I now know that Charles Haughey called a special meeting in Kinsealy the next day to consider what should be done about this "damaging" *Sunday Independent* story. A government Minister was requested to contact my then Editor, the late Michael Hand, to spike the story. Hand, who had not seen the story at that time, agreed to the request.

On Friday October 15th I had arranged to meet a high ranking Garda contact about the Doherty story. A message was delivered to me at my desk in the *Sunday Independent*. It came from the Garda officer's secretary. It stated that I should ring him - but not from my office phone. The message from my garda contact was startling and dramatic. The garda stated that he could not meet me because:

"(1) your phone is tapped;

(2) you are being followed;

(3) every effort will be made to keep your story out of the paper;

(4) the highest person in the country knows what you have."

One of my immediate problems was that I had arranged a lunch time appointment with a then Fianna Fáil Minister who was giving me inside details on the Roscommon affair. I went out the back entrance of the Independent in Middle Abbey Street and was joined by a colleague, Paul Murphy, who is now Editor of the *Drogheda Independent*. I asked Paul to walk with me for a few minutes "but don't ask me what it is all about." We went into Woolworths in Henry Street, left through a side entrance and walked towards O'Connell Street. Paul left me as I entered a side door of Clery's. I took a couple of lifts to the second and third floors and later left through a back entrance. I walked to Wynn's Hotel in Abbey Street, looked in front and behind, and believing that no one had followed me, I entered the Abbey Mooney pub where the Minister was drinking at the counter. I beckoned him to follow me downstairs. There, behind a closed toilet door I told him about the Doherty revelations. The Minister was extremely helpful. He amplified certain matters for me and we parted about 30 minutes later.

I then spent about three hours with the *Sunday Independent* legal department, going through line-by-line my draft of the story with solicitor Michael O'Mahony, who changed about four words in the entire story. I was so delighted that I went to meet Editor Michael Hand in the Oval Bar around 7 p.m. to tell him we had legal clearance. His reply was ominous. Even before he saw the story, he said: "I think we will hold the story, but I will talk to you about it to-morrow."

On Saturday, October 16th, 1982, I showed the story to Michael Hand at 3 p.m. He called me back to his office at 4.30 and in the presence of his deputy, Michael Denieffe, told me that he could not use the story. He said that I was "crucifying" the Minister on flimsy evidence. I replied that the evidence was not flimsy and that five Gardaí were prepared to testify in court in the event of Doherty suing us. We argued for over an hour, with Denieffe helpfully suggesting certain amendments, to which I agreed. Hand refused to agree to the amendments. And when I suggested that there were several follow-up stories to be investigated, he said to put them all into one story – "one big expose!"

I recalled the Garda's warning, "every effort will be made to keep the story out of the paper." I spoke in measured terms to Hand. I told him that I was considering my position as News Editor and thinking of resigning, for I would find it impossible to work with him again. I left the office at 6.30 p.m and made my way to the Fine Gael Ard Fheis in the RDS. Senior members of Fine Gael approached me and asked me if it was true that we were running a big story on Doherty. I refused to confirm the story. An hour later, I was so frustrated I decided to phone the proprietor of Independent Newspapers, Dr. Tony O'Reilly, then the President and Chief Executive of H.J. Heinz. From a neighbour's house at around 10 p.m., I rang him in Pittsburgh and outlined what had happened over the previous week. When I said we got legal clearance to run the story, Dr. O'Reilly asked me to repeat that. I did. He suggested that I should contact the Group Chief Executive of Independent Newspapers, Bartle Pitcher, and make a case to him. The last thing Dr. O'Reilly said to me was: "I will respect your confidence on this."

I later discovered that Dr. O'Reilly was also contacted by the Fine Gael leader, Dr. Garret Fitzgerald, who had been briefed by the then General Secretary of the Garda Sergeants and Inspectors, Derek Nally. And later I learned from *Sunday Independent* political correspondent Joe O'Malley, that he had established the authenticity of my story from independent sources. He told Michael Hand this and added that on foot of publication further individuals would come forward with additional information.

On Sunday, October 17th, 1982, I spent three hours with Mr. Bartle Pitcher who asked me to leave the draft of the story and all the back-up material. That night I went on a journalists golf trip to Liverpool. It was a good time to get out of the country, I felt. And when I returned at 7.30 a.m. the following Wednesday, there was an urgent message from a colleague, John Devine, now the Northern Editor of Independent Newspapers. He said: "Be careful when you come into work – Hand knows you have been on to O'Reilly."

When I arrived at the *Sunday Independent* Hand summoned me to his office. He said that he wanted to talk to me, but first I had to see Joe Hayes, the Managing Director (Ireland): then Liam Healy who was responsible for *Independent Newspapers* world-wide; then Bartle Pitcher, the Group Chief Executive and finally himself. Within two minutes, I faced Joe Hayes who was immediately confrontational, shouting at me from his desk about ten yards away. Initially totally supportive of Michael Hand, he opened up the discussion by saying that if Michael Hand had used that story he would have called for his resignation. I told him about all the back-up evidence from the police, which I had in my possession. All of them, I said, had given written undertakings to testify in court on our behalf. I informed him that the story was cleared legally to run. He was surprised at this and immediately changed his attitude, sitting beside me and putting an arm on my shoulder. "What I am concerned about," he tried to re-assure me, "is your relationship with Michael Hand. How can ye work together?" I told him that I had no confidence in Michael Hand and would find it extremely difficult to work with him.

I left the office of Joe Hayes and knocked at the door of Bartle Pitcher, who was a thorough gentleman, expressing concern for what happened and telling me that he would consider using the story. I asked him if he had any objection to me giving the story to another newspaper, in the event of *Independent Newspapers* not using it. He replied: "Yes, I have; you are an employee of *Independent Newspapers.*"

A few minutes later, I was in the office of Michael Hand, who opened the discussion by telling me that by getting on to Dr.O'Reilly I had undermined his position. He said that I had been totally disloyal to him. I told him that I had vehemently disagreed with his decision not to use the story and as a senior executive of the company I had every right to go over his head. "Yes" he countered, "but you went over four heads to get to O'Reilly." He told me that I was off the story and suspended as News Editor until further notice.

For three weeks, I remained in "limbo" – an outcast. I was treated almost like a North Korean Jew with advanced aids and creeping leprosy! The management of *Independent Newspapers* certainly did not want to know me. Few colleagues even spoke to me. Those who did included Joe O'Malley and Kevin Moore, the father of the chapel of the National Union of Journalists. They were totally supportive. I had committed a cardinal sin. I had spoken to the head honcho – over the heads of four senior executives. They were angry.

Meanwhile, a general election had been called. *Newsweek, The Sunday Times* and several English papers begged me to give them the story. I refused. But when I sought advice from Kevin Moore, he told me to give it to RTE. Helpfully, he argued that the television station was not a rival newspaper. Despite political interference RTE carried the story in a programme called "The Roscommon File" three weeks later. A Government Minister had contacted senior executives in RTE to kill the programme. To their credit, RTE rejected the interfering 'phone call.

After many meetings and soul-searching discussions, a programme called "The Roscommon File" was presented by the current Euro MEP, Pat Cox, produced by Michael Heaney and edited by Donegal-born Joe Mulholland, now the head of RTE Television. The following day, an RTE journalist rang a senior executive in the Independent to tell them how "helpful" I had been in making the programme. A couple of months later, Michael Hand lost his job as Editor and later left to join the *Sunday Tribune*. I was writing a column called Backchat and also doing the difficult job of News Editor. The new Editor, Aengus Fanning, told me that I could not hold on to both jobs. I opted to resign as News Editor and continue with the political column.

A year after the RTE programme, I got a curious call from a Revenue official. He wanted to know why I had not included the fee I received from RTE in my earnings for the previous year. I told him there was a valid reason - I received no fee from RTE. I did not want a fee - I just wanted the story published.

One policeman that I met in Roscommon back in 1982 is now central to the whole affair. Sergeant Dan Sullivan who was then attached to Ballyforan met me in a pub in the village on October 5th. During the brief interview, he was paranoid. We were alone in a large lounge and every couple of minutes when a car passed he immediately stopped talking until he was sure the occupants were not coming into the pub.

What he told me was of paramount significance. The Gardaí in Roscommon were afraid to do their job because of political interference. Before issuing a summons, they virtually had to find out if the people concerned were members of Fianna Fáil. He told me that he was injured in an accident while on duty in Donegal in 1970 and had not received any compensation. The then Minister, Sean Doherty, at one stage told him that he was going to be transferred and that he should pack his bags. Because of that he was hesitant about diligence in his job. He did not want to be transferred. His immediate superiors were friends of Sean Doherty, so he decided to contact the Taoiseach, Mr. Haughey, about the problem.

He added: "I spoke to Mr. Haughey on the telephone at his home. I told him that I was dissatisfied with Mr. Doherty's interference and outlined what had happened." He also told Haughey that he believed that his phone was tapped and that there was widespread phone-tapping in the constituency. According to Sergeant Sullivan, Mr. Haughey told him he "did not want to know about it." According to another Fianna Fáil Minister, Mr. Haughey told Sergeant Sullivan to "outline his complaints in writing."

The fact that Sergeant Sullivan contacted Haughey at that time to tell him of Doherty's political interference with the Roscommon Gardaí and of widespread phone tapping is of major importance. Haughey subsequently denied that he knew anything about journalists phones being tapped in 1982 and strongly refuted allegations that he had seen or been given transcripts of the taps by the former Minister for Justice.

I believe Sergeant Sullivan's version of events – that he briefed Haughey as to what was happening. I also believe that Sean Doherty was telling the truth when he made that bombshell announcement in January 1992. Haughey kept in touch with his Ministers on a regular basis and was fully informed of what was happening in each department. He had to know what was going on in the most sensitive area of all - the Justice department.

There is one other factor that again verifies Sean Doherty's version of events. When the Minister for Justice leaves the country on holidays, the Government is required to have him or her replaced. During his term as Taoiseach, the temporary duties of Minister for Justice were mostly taken over by Mr. Haughey. He took over from Maire Geoghegan Quinn and from her predecessor, Padraig Flynn. When Sean Doherty left Ireland on holidays for France in August 1982, his replacement as Minister was Charles Haughey, who then had access to all police and Department of Justice files, including the files on phone tapping. At that time, the Government officially tapped journalists Bruce Arnold and Geraldine Kennedy.

Politicians, at that time, who believed their phones were tapped included Ministers, Des O'Malley and Dr. Martin O' Donoghue, Roscommon-born Minister of State Terry Leyden, Fianna Fáil TD Ben Briscoe, and Mr. Haughey's former classmate, the late George Colley.

Before I leave 1982 I should point out that I kept a complete dossier on my own personal problems with the *Sunday Independent* and on my three-week investigation in Roscommon. The file included a copy of the story that was spiked by the then Editor, the late Michael Hand. The opening couple of paragraphs read:

"The Minister for Justice Sean Doherty has been involved in widespread interference with the administration of Justice – in particular in the Roscommon area. A *Sunday Independent* investigation over the last three weeks has revealed that he: 'squared' a late drinking prosecution against a publican in Boyle; instructed a Garda not to post a sample in a drunk driving case and harassed Gardaí who were conscientiously doing their job.

"One Garda disclosed that he was afraid of doing his duty 'because of the threat of being transferred'.

"In the drunken driving case in June 1981 involving a lady motorist, Mr. Doherty was then a Junior Minister for Justice. He directed the Garda involved not to post the sample. The member concerned told Mr. Doherty that Sergeant Tom Tully of Boyle was involved in the case. The Minister's reply was "Tom is sound". Sergeant Tully instructed a Garda to post the sample and requested that Mr. Doherty be informed that any further contact on the matter should be made with himself. Sergeant Tully was not contacted subsequently by Mr. Doherty. The case went to court and the lady was convicted and disqualified from driving."

Some years before the Haughey revelations, Sean Doherty had serious financial problems. Irish Nationwide Building Society issued a writ against him for non-payment of his mortgage. The case was settled on the doorstep of Boyle court. After Charles Haughey was deposed, Sean Doherty's financial affairs changed dramatically. According to the Dáil manifesto, Sean Doherty owns land at Knocknacarrow, Cootehall, Boyle, used for letting. He was given planning permission by Roscommon County Council to build three two-storey houses at

Knocknacarrow. He owned three properties in Dublin - No 4 Woodlane, No 7 Clifton Court, Ellis Quay and property at Dillon Place. They are all used for letting. He also owned three half-acre sites, one without planning and one with planning permission for a marina. He owned another site on which two chalets were built.

All TDs and Senators are now required to declare their financial interests.

6

THE DUNNES
STORES
PAYMENTS

The revelation that Ben Dunne gave Haughey £1 million sparked the first (McCracken) Tribunal which was given the task of looking into payments to politicians. But the subsequent Moriarty Tribunal found that Dunne's generosity had been even greater than that. More interesting was the timing of the first payment to Haughey. McCracken found £185,000 sterling in December 1987, from which it was concluded that Des Traynor had approached Dunne for funds around November of that year. But the discovery by Moriarty of £282,500 sterling drawn on Dunnes Stores in Bangor, County Down, and dated May 1987 changed the timetable. Ben Dunne said he could not remember authorising the cheque. But he accepted the evidence that he had done so and that Traynor's approach had probably come a few months before that, around February 1987.

Dunnes Stores executive Matt Price testified that Ben Dunne had told him to make a cheque payable to Tripleplan Ltd. and send it to the company accountant and trustee, Noel Fox. The directors of Tripleplan were Cayman Island bankers the late John Furze and John Collins, who handled Traynor's Cayman accounts. The potential significance of the timing was that the election on February 17th, 1987 made it near certain that Haughey would become Taoiseach again. On March 10th, he was so elected by the Dáil.

Dunne testified that Traynor had approached Noel Fox looking for donations for Haughey, who appeared to be in severe financial difficulty. Within two or three weeks of the approach, Dunne decided he would put up all the money, rather than be part of a "consortium". The money would be paid over a period of six to seven months and would have to be handled delicately and privately because of Haughey's political status. Dunne told the Tribunal the money was to come from a trading company in the Far East. Some time later, however, Fox told him that Haughey needed the money quickly. He remembered being asked to "get a cheque quick" and he accepted that this must have been the Tripleplan cheque.

Dunne maintained that he never thought of the donations as his own money, but as Dunnes Stores money, which somewhat contradicted the impression of impetuous generosity given at the McCracken Tribunal. But in his then position of sole authority in the company, he did not see much difference. "I thought of it as all the one," he said.

Faced with these mysteries, Tribunal lawyer John Coughlan SC asked Noel Fox if he could think of anything significant that occurred in relation to Dunnes Stores in early or mid-1987, but Fox could not recall anything.

The Tribunal summoned two former chairmen of the Revenue Commissioners to give evidence. One of them, Philip Curran, told how Haughey called him to his office in 1988 and asked if he would meet Ben Dunne. Haughey said Dunnes Stores were making a lot of money but he thought there was some problem about the family trust and capital taxation. Curran said he would have agreed to meet Dunne anyway. When they did meet, Dunne had talked about the accumulating tax liability in the trust but it was not clear what he wanted and nothing came of the meeting. Another Commissioner, Cathal MacDomhnaill, testified that the Revenue had raised an assessment on the Dunnes Trust in 1987. This was appealed and in 1988 the Appeals Commissioner found in favour of the trustees and overturned the assessment. He said that, after taking legal advice, the Revenue decided not to further appeal this decision.

7

MILLIONAIRE LIFESTYLE ON A DEPUTY'S WAGES

When confronted in 1997 at the McCracken Tribunal, Charles Haughey stated emphatically that he did not enjoy an expensive lifestyle. The Tribunal at that time was investigating payments totalling £2m. made by businessman Ben Dunne to him and to former Fine Gael Minister Michael Lowry. Questioned by Denis McCullough, counsel for the Tribunal, he said: "My work was my lifestyle and when I was in office I worked every day, all day. There was no room for any sort of an extravagant lifestyle."

It has now emerged from financial records submitted to the Moriarty Tribunal, which is investigating payments made by several businessmen to Mr. Haughey, that the former Taoiseach spent almost £3m. on day-to-day expenses between 1988 and 1996. The personal outlay averaged £26,470 a month between 1988 and 1996. Haughey's only visible source of income during those years was his salary as Taoiseach and his state pension. In 1988, he earned £38, 465 as Taoiseach, plus his TDs salary of less than £30,000.

Documentation given to the Moriarty Tribunal about Haughey's personal expenses in fact reflected a lavish lifestyle. They include large bills each month from some of Dublin's most expensive restaurants. People close to Mr. Haughey during those years were well aware of the high flying style to which he became accustomed, and of the amount of money he had to spend to sustain it. His pursuit of extravagance in his early years as Taoiseach brought him to the finest stores and eateries in Europe and America. While he was warning the Dáil in the autumn of 1987 that the country was on a "slippery slide to disaster," the seamstresses of Charvet in Paris, were stitching his initials on sea island shirts at £800 each and suits costing £3,000. He still has his name on several bolts of fabric there and his measurements are kept in a vault. Like royalty from all over the world, a phone call can produce these exclusive creations and to a perfect fit. The clientele included the late French President, Francois Mitterand, Teddy Kennedy, the Aga Khan, Saddam Hussein, most of the Arab Royals and even Prince Charles. In the past, other illustrious shoppers at Charvet included John F. Kennedy, the Duke of Windsor and Mr. Haughey's hero, none other than Napoleon Bonaparte. (On one occasion, during a visit to the home of journalist, Noelle Campbell Sharpe, CJ specially asked to be left alone while he spent some time in her "Napoleon" room, soaking up the atmosphere and imbibing the vibes). Always immaculately dressed, Mr. Haughey kept his Michael Scott-designed mahogany wardrobes in Kinsealy fitted with expensive flannels, blazers, suits and personalised shirts. Abrahamson's in South Anne Street, Dublin, was one of the few Irish establishments permitted to make his suits.

Over the years, Charles Haughey has gradually surrounded himself with the expensive toys that are the hallmark of international high fliers. Apart from his 10 bedroom Georgian mansion at Kinsealy standing on 270 acres, he also has a splendid retreat on his own island at Inishvickillane, off the coast of County Kerry. He moved into Kinsealy in 1969, after selling his former home and lands at Grangemore in Raheny for £200,000 on which he made a profit of £150,000 on what he had bought it for nine years before. He bought "Abbeyville", Kinsealy for £120,000 which equates to £1.2m at 1999 values. Haughey was Minister for Finance at the time, earning a TDs salary of £3,500 and a ministerial allowance of £2,500.

The Chief Revenue Commissioner for Dublin commissioned the Gandon-designed mansion at Kinsealy in the 18th century. Surrounded by extensive parkland, a lake, swimming pool, ornamental fountains, boathouse, stables, orchard, a helicopter pad, a pair of ice houses, a 200-year-old dairy and a 20-foot sculpture of the mythical Irish hero Cuchulainn, it is a breeding centre for horses, red deer and Irish wolfhounds. It produces its own non-commercial honey and is a sanctuary for pheasant, duck and swans.

Within the house, Charles Haughey eases away the vicissitudes of life in an Italian marble bathtub. The ballroom boasts the finest Gandon interior in Ireland. His home is filled with busts of himself and some priceless paintings by Jack Yeats, Louis Le Brocquy, Nathaniel Hone, Edward Maguire, Basil Blackshaw and Tom Ryan. They hang easily in elegant rooms filled with period furniture, collections of fine books, French porcelain horses, and a rare 1916 Proclamation hanging in the Billiard Room.

Here, the Kinsealy Squire has entertained Francois Mitterand, Luciano Pavorotti, Canada's former Prime Minister Brian Mulrooney, Australia's former PM Bob Hawke, Lord Snowdon, and the family of his favourite politician Mikhail Gorbachev. They were all treated to a tipple in his full-sized and well-stocked Irish theme bar. Vintage wines are stored in the cellar, and there guests sampled Chateau Lafite 1920 (£300 a bottle), Chateau Mouton Rothschild '67 and Chateau Margaux '57 (up to £1,000 a bottle), Chateau d'Yquem (£500 for a bottle of the '75), Roederer Cristal Champagne (£85 for the '90 vintage) and his favourite, Chateau Latour (£150 a bottle of the Haut Brion '86).   Abbeyville itself is conservatively valued at £10m. It is reckoned it will be rezoned for housing in the next five or six years when its realisable value could be up to £100m.

Haughey bought his island Inishvickillane, off the Blaskets in Kerry for £25,000 in 1974 – when his TDs salary was £5,000. Notable for its Christian monastic oratory and a seabird colony of 12 species on 171 acres of rocky Atlantic coastline, it is valued at £3m. When he had an architect-designed single-storey ranch-style stone house built there, construction materials had to be hauled-slung under the bellies of powerful helicopters across a nine-mile stretch of treacherous seas that separates it from the mainland. His guests on the island included Mitterand and Senator Ted Kennedy. When President Mitterand visited, there was nearly an international incident. The French insisted that the President's food would be tasted before it was served to him. Haughey made everybody happy by eating it first himself.

He also owns a detached holiday home in County Wexford originally built for his daughter, Eimear. And he has another secluded bungalow at Lislarry in County Sligo, a couple of miles from Rosses Point, which is used regularly by his brother, Fr. Eoin Haughey, for golfing breaks. The combined value of the properties in Wexford and Sligo is estimated at £300,000.

His favourite mode of transport is a 60-foot steel-hulled motor sailer Celtic Mist that provides immense pleasure for him as he tests his sailing skills against the elements in the British Isles and at Brittany in France, his favourite spot. Bought in the Mediterranean after his last boat crashed off the rocks of Mizzen Head in the 1980s, when Mr. Haughey had a very lucky escape, the Dutch-built Celtic Mist would cost more than £250,000 if bought new to-day, and even second hand, is still worth £120,000. It is kept at the exclusive marina in Malahide in North Dublin, where the annual berthing fee is £4,000 – or £42,000 to buy a berth outright. Celtic Mist has always had a professional skipper, and with insurance, repairs, maintenance and fuel, is reckoned to cost about £25,000 annually to keep seaworthy. In 1998, it required a new engine, costing nearly £30,000. A decade ago, it underwent a total re-fit at Crosshaven Boat Yard in County Cork.

Mr. Haughey has access to his son's three helicopters in Celtic Helicopters. Nevertheless, when he became Taoiseach, he lost no time procuring a Gulfstream jet aircraft - the ultimate millionaire's accessory – but paid for by the Government and the taxpayer.

Then there were the racehorses. In the early days, the late Dick McCormick trained The Chaser and Miss Cossie for him and Tom Dreaper schooled the jumper Vulforo. His most famous hunter was Flashing Steel which had the distinction of winning the Irish Grand National at Fairyhouse. He bought the gelding in 1990 for £120,000 - when his Taoiseach's salary was £67,174. Even though the horse made more than £100,000, it still did not earn its keep. Mr. Haughey ordered his own hunting pinks for riding, and a life-size portrait of him in full hunting regalia used to hang in the main hall in Kinsealy.

His generosity to his family, his constituents and intimate circle of friends is legendary. He was a regular shopper at Cartier, Tiffanys and Louis Vuitton. He rarely returned from overseas trips without some magnificent gifts. On one occasion he bought a very large bottle of expensive perfume and a small one, leading to speculation as to who would get the bigger one and who the smaller.

He was the recipient of some superb gifts during his term of office. His pride and joy was the controversial dagger and diamonds from an Arab Sheikh. He is equally proud of the hand-stitched saddle that Col. Gadaffi gave him. He had gifts of rare books, antique silver, paintings by the dozen and some excellent crystal.

Over the years, he has become a connoisseur of superb vintage wines and excellent food. During his many trips around the world, he never missed an opportunity to partake of the best restaurants everywhere. In the south of France, he has stayed over the years in the same lavish suite at the Carlton, though when he and his wife Maureen honeymooned there over 40 years before they opted for a more modest double room. In the Carlton and Le Colombe d'Or in Saint Paul de Venice, there is an open reservation and a table waiting. Le Colombe d'Or has a treasured supply of Chateau Petrus - a snip at £600 a bottle. In London, Le Gavoche has come to know all his favourites vintages and in New York, Le Grenouille on East 52nd Street - one of the most expensive restaurants in Manhattan - was his No 1 spot. In Dublin, over the years, he has frequented the private dining room in Locks on the Grand Canal, the King Citric overlooking Howth Bay and Dobbins in the city centre. But his favourite eatery in the capital was the John Howard owned, Le Coq Hardi, a restaurant brimful of memories for himself and his mistress of the last 27 years, columnist Terry Keane.

When Charles Haughey became Taoiseach in December 1979, his faithful political buddy Brian Lenihan pleaded with him to end the relationship with Terry. "It is not appropriate for you as Taoiseach," Lenihan told him. Haughey ignored the advice.

8

EVEN THE CHANDELIERS WERE SHAKING!

CJ and Terry met at least twice a week at Le Coq Hardi restaurant in Dublin. When Haughey arrived, proprietor John Howard and his wife, Catherine, personally greeted him. There was a special peck on the cheek for Catherine as they made their way to the private dining room upstairs. Only the staff would see them in this magnificent Georgian room, with its superb fireplace. Overlooking Pembroke Road, it had sliding doors, a table, chairs and a couch. In this special upstairs place, the pair had total privacy. Staff only entered the room if they were called.

The staff was well used to all their gestures. When Terry wanted more wine, she tipped her glass to the waiter; CJ simply raised a hand. Most of the time they were discreet, but on a number of occasions they were seen by staff holding hands. On one occasion Terry was desperately trying to close the sliding doors for a late night canoodle and had to have help from a waiter. Before CJ left at night, staff said they had a little snogging session. And then there was that special night remembered by everybody present – the night the chandeliers shook!

The bill was never less than £300 and the staff at the Dublin eatery in Pembroke Road estimated that the weekly bill was never less than £1,000. No money was ever paid by Mr. Haughey at the Dublin restaurant. In fact, he hardly ever saw a bill there. It was invoiced to him at Government buildings and paid on a monthly basis.

We have established that Charles Haughey paid the bills from his own personal account. We wrote firstly to the Office of the Comptroller and Auditor General, Mr. John Purcell, and asked if he was aware if bills for the period August 1 1988 to December 31 1996 were paid personally by Mr. Haughey or did they come from public funds. During this period, financial records revealed that he spent £26,470 a month. In reply, Mr. Fergus O'Brien, Private Secretary to the Comptroller wrote: "This Office audits the expenditure charged to the Annual Accounts on a test basis and any serious breach of regularity/propriety would be brought to the attention of the Comptroller and Auditor General. If he deems it appropriate to do so, he may include a reference to the issue in his report to Dáil Eireann. I can confirm that there was no such reference to the former Taoiseach's expenses in the period mentioned in your letter. It may well be that the Department of the Taoiseach can provide the information sought by you and I would suggest that you might contact that Department in this regard."

We did. The reply from Ann Whelan, Head of Finance Unit at the Department of the Taoiseach read: "I wish to advise you that, in the period 1987 to February 1992, the records of the Department show one payment to Le Coq Hardi Restaurant – for a lunch hosted by the former Taoiseach on December 4 1991 for the British Prime Minister, in Government Buildings."

When Terry Keane dined in the Coq Hardi, she sometimes ordered a case of vintage wine. It is not known who paid for it. Several times Terry dined with her own friends. On one memorable occasion, she invited the eldest daughter of the late Gus Martin, a UCD professor, to dine with her. The lunch came to £45 and the drink to £450! The bill was invoiced to Mr. Haughey.

Terry had expensive tastes. She loved lobster, but Charlie preferred oysters the French way - a little vinegar, baby onions and lemon. CJ was also partial to asparagus. For main course, he would generally choose fish – either monkfish or sole. He never ate desert. Terry frequently did.

Terry would start lunch with Dom Perignon (at least £100 a bottle) and a packet of Marlboro cigarettes. Charlie, who fancied himself as a connoisseur of vintage wine, would begin with Poullign Monrachet White 80. And for dinner he generally chose

Calon de Seque Bordeaux. After the wine, he drank claret. While CJ always arrived early to avoid the crowd, he left promptly after midnight. Terry would generally stay until 4 or 5 a.m., drinking Muscat de Beaume de Venise.

On another memorable night, Charlie left as usual shortly after 12. He and Terry were dining in the private room with a media editor and his girl friend. The girl friend left for a short while to go to the powder room. Terry made the most of it. She was seen by the staff groping the Editor. A member of staff saw them passionately French kissing.

His guests included people like Nobel Prize winner Seamus Heaney and the glamourous Travel Director Gillian Bowler. Terry sometimes brought an entourage, which included family and friends.

Within one 24-hour period, there were three Taoisigh in the Coq Hardi. CJ and Terry were dining in the private room; the man who succeeded him as Prime Minister, Albert Reynolds, was downstairs with a party; and in another room the next night, Albert's successor, Bertie Ahern, was dining with some friends.

Staff remember another special night at Le Coq Hardi. It was an autumn evening in September and CJ was celebrating his 69th birthday. Terry's present was thought-provoking and audacious. It was a painting of a mermaid lying on a bed. CJ was in no doubt that the mermaid was Terry in a sexy rear view pose. The lady had style. Haughey liked to be served by a French speaking waiter, for he is himself fluent in French. His usual tip for lunch was £10, and for dinner £20.

But their regular get togethers were not confined to the Coq Hardi. They also had the use of a tastefully furnished mews in Wellington Road. CJ had given the owner a tax break when he was Minister for Finance and had access to it. They also used a place near the Berkeley Hotel and a mews called "The Pink Palace" at Uplands, Annamoe, County Wicklow, formerly owned by a German Count Franz Waldburg. They made use of the place usually in the middle of the week. Terry insisted on fresh flowers before they arrived in separate cars.

The Berkeley Court in Ballsbridge was another favourite haunt. Thanks to his excellent relationship with the owner, the late P.V. Doyle, CJ had the use of a suite which he and Terry frequented at least once a week. The bill for the fare they enjoyed there was between £300 and £600 per week and sometimes as high as £1,000. The former Taoiseach operated a similar arrangement to Le Coq Hardi. The bill was never sent to his home in Kinsealy but posted to his office at Government buildings, and no bill was ever sent without first being vetted by the proprietor himself. According to Ann Whelan, head of Finance Unit at the Department of the Taoiseach, no payment by the Department was made to the Berkeley Court on behalf of Mr. Haughey.

Similar to the arrangements in Le Coq Hardi, Terry Keane brought her own entourage to the Berkeley Court. She regularly ordered cases of wine. Again it is not known whether she paid for it herself. After the retirement of the former Taoiseach, the *Sunday Independent* columnist was seldom seen in the hotel.

There were numerous trips together out of Ireland. They visited France on many occasions. But it was unusual for the Taoiseach to have non-Government personnel aboard the Government jet. This came about after a row between Haughey and his Minister for Finance, Albert Reynolds. The Department of Finance was in charge of the Government jet. Any non-Government personnel had to be cleared by Finance. Albert Reynolds brought a party of journalists on the jet to Milan during Ireland's EC Presidency and when Haughey heard about it, he almost blew a fuse. He told Reynolds that the jet was for him and could only be used by other Ministers in "special circumstances". CJ kicked up such a fuss that Reynolds told him to take total charge of the jet. In future, the Taoiseach's office would clear all non-Government personnel. While it was a headache for CJ to have to oversee its use, it meant that he could bring anybody he wanted to aboard without any questions being asked. Friends recall Terry ringing home on one occasion from the exclusive George V Hotel in Paris. She told them that she was using a circular bed and had difficulty finding her head! While she was on the phone, she said CJ was in the shower.

At Charvet, he bought silk dressing gowns. Terry admired them so much that he brought six of them back to her after his next visit to Paris. During that visit, his then Foreign Minister, Brian Lenihan accompanied him. The other members of his entourage included his late private secretary, Padraig O Hanrachain and Government Press Secretary, Frank Dunlop. After their brief visit to the then President of France, Giscard d'Estang, they were free for the rest of the afternoon. CJ announced to his colleagues: "We are going shopping!" At the entrance to Charvet's, they were met by the Patron and escorted to a plush waiting area. A couple of moments later, CJ came out with parcels. And when Frank Dunlop looked closely at him, he said: "They are my shirts, Frank." To the amusement of his colleagues, who included the Foreign Minister Lenihan, CJ pointed to them and gesticulated to the Patron, explaining "They are my security." In honour of the occasion, Charlie's "security" men were presented with a silk tie each.

Terry was also given Louis Vuitton luggage – six matching suitcases worth £3,000. Money was sent to Paris the next day to pay for the purchase, which Terry still uses. On one occasion in New York, a Bord Failte executive paid for Terry's flight and her hotel.

Terry Keane used her friendship with influential friends when she got into any scrape. She had a minor brush with the law in Stephen's Green, near Leeson Street in Dublin where the car she was travelling in was stopped by a garda. The car was driven by *Irish Independent* columnist, Angela Phelan, and he asked for her driving licence and insurance. As Angela was fumbling in her handbag, a voice from the back seat said: "Why don't you tell him to fuck off!" The garda promptly took out his notebook. As he peered into the back of the car, a woman's voice, clearly inebriated, added: "Don't you know I am the most powerful woman in the country?" The young policeman put away his notebook and told the driver to move on.

When CJ had money, he was very generous. But when he was out of office, he had to be more careful about his spending. On one occasion, after Terry moved to fashionable Ranelagh in Dublin South, she told CJ: "I have to have an alarm system." CJ had an elaborate system installed for £3,500. On an other occasion, her car did not start. She phoned CJ: "I need a car and I need it now." At the time, he was out of office – all he could afford was a secondhand Renault 5.

Terry was involved in a freak accident when a lighted match

singed her eyebrow and she was taken to St. Vincent's Hospital. The only bed available was in a public ward, which did not please her. She phoned CJ who told her to try to move to the Mater Hospital on the north side of Dublin, because he had "no pull" at St. Vincent's. Terry rang her husband, Ronan Keane, a High Court Judge. He told her: "We are trying to have you moved." She quickly countered: "You are not trying hard enough!" When fellow patients attempted to talk to her, she pulled her curtain across, saying: "We have nothing in common." She complained so much about the "dreadful people" she was with and it became so bad that Haughey arranged for lunch to be sent from the fashionable Patrick Gilbaud restaurant. She eventually got a private ward. One of her first visitors was businessman Gerry Jones, a tall man with a black patch over his eye and a close friend of Haughey. Gerry moved out of his chair when CJ arrived. He offered the chair, but Charlie refused. Then Mr. Haughey, always conscious of his small stature, could not contain himself: "I know you are taller than I am; there is no need to rub it in."

While in hospital, Terry complained about the television set, which was coin operated. She told CJ she wanted one of her own, a white one. A cream one arrived and she kicked up another row. She fired a tray at the TV saying: "I said I wanted a white one." That TV went back to her house. When husband Ronan Keane asked her where she got it, she told him: "Noelle Campbell Sharpe got a present of it and gave it to me."

During a holiday in the Canaries, Terry was involved in another freak accident. Part of a stainless steel covering had come loose and she tripped on it and sustained a nasty cut in her leg. She was rushed to an American clinic in Puerto Rico. It was crudely sewn up with black gut. Later on the phone to CJ she sobbed: "My ankles are my crowning glory; and they are ruined!" CJ got on to the then head of Aer Rianta, Martin Dully, and asked him to arrange a wheelchair at Dublin airport for her return. Meanwhile, Terry was busy in the Canaries, loading a canvas bag with bottles of liquor. When the jet arrived at Dublin Airport, she was first to disembark. Husband Ronan was there to greet her and wheeled her off. He escorted her through customs, a rug cleverly concealing the bag of booze!

A Terry Keane put down could be devastating. During the wilderness years, after Taoiseach Jack Lynch sacked him, close friend P.J. Mara drove CJ around the country. A rendezvous with Terry had been arranged and Mara joined them for a few minutes. In a frosty voice, Terry told Haughey: "Tell your driver to wait in the car!" She also had a minor brush with Charlie's son, Ciaran, who was at the time seeing a Danish beauty. Terry told Charlie: "Keep your son and his Danish hairdresser out of my social circle!"

Haughey was not Terry's only beau. She had a relationship with a former Government Minister. Her first child – a girl called Jane – was given up for adoption in England and many years later the girl wrote to her mother asking to meet her. Terry subsequently talked at length on television about Jane and the emotion of their reunion, and how Jane was warmly welcomed into the family.

Terry Keane has since claimed that an actor, Jimmy Donnelly, with whom she had a love affair in the Sixties after a row with her then regular boyfriend, barrister Ronan Keane, was Jane's father. She claims the pregnancy happened when she fell into Donnelly's arms on the rebound.

But her story of who fathered her daughter in the *Sunday Times* is very much at variance with a dramatic incident that took place in the lobby of the Shelbourne Hotel in Dublin after Jane had come to live in Dublin in the late eighties.

The pair of them were having coffee when a tall, dark-haired man walked into the lobby. Terry recognised him as Limerick-born Daragh O'Malley, the actor son of the late Donogh O'Malley, flamboyant and legendary Minister for Education. Terry admits that she was friendly with the late Minister, but this friendship did not extend to an affair.

Daragh, who is based in Los Angeles, was polite when she called him over. Then she introduced him to the young lady with her: "Meet your step-sister."

Daragh confirmed this to me when I started to write this book and repeated the incident to me since the *Sunday Times* story on the actor Jimmy Donnelly. The two versions cannot be reconciled. Either Terry Keane lied to Daragh O'Malley in the Shelbourne Hotel when she led him to believe that Jane was his half-sister, or she lied to the *Sunday Times*.

"It happened in the Shelbourne Hotel," Daragh insists. "She claimed that Donogh (his father, and uncle of former Minister and Progressive Democrats leader Des O'Malley) was the girl's father."

Jane, whose adoptive English parents were called de Burgh, worked for a period in the *Sunday Tribune* newspaper. She later married Dublin-born Carl Carpenter and they have a family.

Terry Keane spent a lot of time with her neighbours, the late Professor Gus Martin and his wife, Claire. On one occasion late at night, she rang her "Sweetie", Haughey. "Your response to Margaret Thatcher in the Dáil to-day was superb," she said. Then turning to Gus Martin and covering the mouthpiece, she whispered: "What did Charlie actually say?" Then there was the night Charlie accompanied the late Gus Martin and his wife to the Abbey Theatre. Gus was Chairman of the National Theatre and had been pleading for years with Mr. Haughey, a keen supporter of the Arts, to see an Abbey play. They were watching the John B. Keane play "The Field", with the late Ray McAnally in the role of Bull McCabe, the central character. After the first act, Gus remarked that Mr. Haughey would empathise with the main character after the interval.

"You will see the greed and avarice of this bully in the second period," he said.

"What do you mean," said Charlie, "I am with this character right from the opening act."

9

WHERE THE HAUGHEY MONEY CAME FROM

Haughey's wealth had always been a source of fascination and conjecture. It was obvious that he lived far beyond the style that could be supported by a politician's salary, even a Taoiseach's. The journalist Vincent Browne regularly asked Haughey at press conferences if he could explain the source of his wealth, to which the answer was always a dismissive, "Ask my bank manager." Many people believed that Haughey was a very shrewd and lucky investor, and as a result was probably a wealthy man. What was known was that he had set up his own accountancy practice with his chum Harry Boland in 1950. The firm was apparently successful. He had also sold his original house, Grangemore, with 45 acres of land, to the Gallagher Group builders, in 1969. With the proceeds he bought Abbeville, with 250 acres, at Kinsealy, near the coastal town of Malahide north of the City. He made a profit of £84,000 on the move to his new home. Two years later he sold a small parcel of his new land to building materials company Cement Roadstone for £130,000. These were hefty sums before the oil crisis inflation of the 1970s. But even with this money, it was generally thought that Haughey would have had to have played volatile financial markets better than most professionals if he was to acquire the kind of wealth he so conspicuously displayed.

The other possibility, widely believed, was that Haughey was "on the inside" on various property deals, because of his friendships with builders and developers.

This was a period of rapid economic expansion, of a kind not seen until the present boom. There was a huge demand for housing and a fortune to be made from buying the potential development land. A politician with the right connections, like Haughey, could share in that. It might not even be improper to do so, provided no use was made of government information or abuse of power to deliberately change policy for such personal gain.

It now transpires that the trappings of wealth and gracious living surrounding Mr. Haughey were a sham. By the mid-1980s, far from being wealthy, Haughey appeared to be broke and it was his need for money that led, in the end, to the destruction of his reputation. It may never be known how he came to be in dire straits. There were stories that he had lost out in the stock market, or punting on Irish oil exploration shares. One story is that he had to rescue a close friend who was a "name" at Lloyd's insurance market who could not meet her liabilities incurred in one of the syndicates. But perhaps the real reason is that his spending grossly exceeded his income, from whatever sources. That would not be surprising, given that he had added to his possessions, and his liabilities, with the purchase of Inishvickillane in the Blasket Islands and the expensive construction of a house on it.

Haughey's overdraft in the AIB branch in Dame Street, where he had held a personal account for many years, reached £1 million, and the bank was seriously worried. The problem was referred to a four-man sub-committee that looked at "sensitive accounts" in the bank. Since this one belonged to a Taoiseach, sensitive was certainly the word. But AIB decided they could not ignore an overdraft of this size and threatened legal action if Haughey did not pay it off. He received a letter to that effect, signed by no less a person than the AIB chief executive, the late Niall Crowley.

Haughey handed the matter over to Des Traynor who, as we now know, handled all his financial transactions. Traynor, who had become a partner the first day he joined Haughey Boland as a qualified accountant, was then managing director of Guinness & Mahon, a small Irish merchant bank. Traynor negotiated that AIB would write off half the money owed. From AIB's point of view this was not such a bad deal, since it avoided damaging publicity and the bank might not have secured any more from legal action. Guinness & Mahon provided a £500,000 loan to Haughey for the balance and became his personal bankers.

The method of payment was quintessential Haughey. He arranged to meet a senior executive of AIB at the door of bank headquarters in Ballsbridge. His car drew up and Haughey handed the £500,000 bank draft through the passenger window, as though to a tradesman, before driving off.

Guinness & Mahon were a subsidiary of Guinness Mahon in London. The parent bank was horrified when it discovered that a £500,000 loan had been given to a customer whose known income was less than £100,000 a year. A ferocious row ensued and six months later Traynor left as joint managing director of the bank and some believed his departure was connected to the Haughey loan. However, he later returned as chairman of the bank. One reason may have been that the system he established for offshore accounts was a major source of business for a small bank that was beginning to look out of place in the changing financial world.

This was the system Haughey used to fund his lifestyle. In essence, it was simplicity itself, but so designed as to be surrounded by a near-impenetrable wall of secrecy. Haughey's personal secretary in Kinsealy would send the bills to a company called BEL Services. Jack Stakelum, an accountant who did his articles under Haughey in the firm of Haughey Boland, ran this company. Stakelum got the money through Guinness & Mahon bank and later Irish Intercontinental Bank, and paid the bills. But the ultimate source of the money was the so-called "Ansbacher" accounts in the Cayman Islands.

This system was operated by Padraig Colleary, a banking software expert who, at the time, was an associate director of G&M. In the late 1980s, the Ansbacher accounts in the Caymans held almost £38 million, belonging to a variety of unknown individuals. Mr. Colleary kept the records of individual accounts within the Caymans bank; how much was deposited into each and how much was withdrawn. These individual details were held in a "bureau system" which meant access was restricted to Colleary. Not even senior officials of the bank could check them.

In any case, there was only a code number for each account, and no names of account holders. The bank's auditors were also unable to gain access to the account details held in the bureau system. They accepted this on the basis that the accounts were really the business of Ansbacher Ltd in the Caymans rather than G&M. Also there was every reason to believe that Colleary was meticulous in his record-keeping so that there was nothing to concern auditors of the bank.

Colleary in turn was acting under the instructions of Des Traynor, who in effect handled Haughey's private finances, and John Furze, the banker who was the link to the accounts in the Caymans. The system was already in place before Colleary joined G&M in 1974. Traynor operated as chief executive of the bank, and was chairman of the Cayman Islands' bank. Because Colleary's duties included the maintenance of all customer accounts in the bank, the "memorandum accounts," which recorded the Cayman Island transactions became his responsibility. Traynor moved to become chairman of building materials group CRH in 1986, but the system continued. It operated even after Colleary left G&M in 1989 and when the Dublin accounts were transferred to Irish Intercontinental Bank. Traynor would send the instructions for movements of money to the bank. Colleary would get a copy of these, so that he could adjust the memorandum accounts accordingly. The crucial difference was that the bank was told only which account to pay money into from the general Ansbacher deposits – Colleary was instructed which of the Ansbacher accounts to debit, i.e. whose money was being used.

Clearly, money going into BEL Services to pay Haughey's bills was coming from the Cayman deposits held on Haughey's behalf. After Traynor died in 1994, Colleary and Furze transferred the files relating to the Cayman deposits from the CRH offices in Fitzwilliam Street to offices belonging to Sam Field Corbett. He was also an associate of Traynor and Haughey and operated a company called Management and Investment Services Ltd. the company to which bank statements relating to the accounts were sent.

Ultimately, bank confidentiality laws of the Cayman Islands guaranteed the secrecy of the Ansbacher accounts. The names of the account holders were not available anywhere in Ireland – that information is held in the Caymans' bank. Even more importantly, the details of the payments into the accounts, which would give information on how much money Haughey received and when he received it, are locked behind Cayman Islands' law.

10

FLYING AROUND
IN GOLDEN
CIRCLES

The revelations at the Moriarty Tribunal about Celtic Helicopters identified for the first time some of the people who made up the golden circle that surrounded Mr. Haughey.

In the course of tracing money emanating from the supermarket boss Ben Dunne, the Tribunal saw £180,000 making its way towards Charles Haughey. £80,000 went into Ansbacher deposits for Mr. Haughey's benefit. The remaining £100,000 appeared to go into Celtic Helicopters, the company set up in 1985 by Haughey's son, Ciaran and his partner, John Barnacle, another helicopter pilot. In tracing this money, the Tribunal came across another £100,000. This led to a full probe of Celtic Helicopters. The Tribunal learned that Charles Haughey met the former Labour TD Dr. John O'Connell in March 1985, shortly after he joined Fianna Fáil. Haughey asked his new party colleague for a contribution of £5,000 for Celtic Helicopters. And in the witness box at the Tribunal, Dr. O'Connell said he did it because he thought everyone was making similar contributions.

In one of the most bizarre tales, he informed the Tribunal that CJH told him he was asking some friends to make contributions to his son Ciaran's fledging helicopter company. He asked O'Connell straight up for a £5,000 contribution and inquired if he had any friends who might do likewise. Dr. O'Connell, who had a pathological fear of flying, was told: "If ever you want a lift in a helicopter please let us know."

Then for some unexplained reason in 1992, Charles Haughey

wanted to buy back O'Connell's shares, even though the doctor was blissfully unaware at that time that he ever was a shareholder in Celtic Helicopters. He was also aware that Celtic Helicopters was not a thriving enterprise. Haughey informed the bemused doctor that his "once-off payment" was in fact an investment in some shares, though he was never issued with a share certificate. O'Connell decided to play hard ball over the shares and asked for £15,000. Haughey agreed immediately and Dr. O'Connell was puzzled for he knew that the shares were almost worthless at that time. Dr. O'Connell revealed that they shook hands on the deal the day Haughey resigned as Taoiseach in 1992. He was quite sad – Dr. O'Connell noticed tears in his eyes.

Months later – after Celtic Helicopters had received a solicitor's letter demanding the doctor's share certificate – Haughey summoned Dr. O'Connell and gave him £15,000 at the Dublin North selection convention, where Haughey's son, Sean, was to win a nomination. There was no exchange of share certificates – because the Doctor had never received any.

Dr. O'Connell was asked for the contribution from Charles Haughey less than two months after he joined the party. He said he presumed that a lot of members of Fianna Fáil had been asked for a similar contribution. That statement was revealing in itself. It spoke of a political culture where money moved easily between politicians. No questions asked. No answers given.

In 1985, Charles Haughey "cornered" the former DG of Bord Failte, Joe Malone, meat baron Seamus Purcell and his close friend, wealthy hotelier P.V. Doyle, who between them took a 40pc stake in Celtic Helicopters. Haughey also received substantial contribution from Cruse Moss, an American businessman, who subsequently won contracts for building CIE buses. The investment would have been insignificant to Moss, who has endowed a couple of engineering professorships in Ohio University. He got his money back from Celtic, as did Dr. John O'Connell.

Former Bord Failte director general Joe Malone told the Tribunal how he became involved in contributing to Celtic Helicopters. He said he had spent 50 years in the tourism business and back in 1984-85 Charles Haughey asked him if he would like to become involved in the helicopter company his son was setting up. As a director of Aer Lingus at the time, he declined because of a perceived conflict of interest.

The then Fianna Fáil leader was determined that Celtic would have a prestigious Chairman, so he asked his friend, Joe Malone.

In his evidence to the Tribunal, Malone said he felt the former Taoiseach was offended at his earlier refusal to become chairman of the company. Because of a friendship between his son, Joseph Junior, and Ciaran Haughey, he decided to invest £15,000, specifying that it would be in Joe Junior's name. He said he was later asked for additional investment but he declined. The initial investment remained in his son's name.

Asked how he came to the decision to invest, Mr. Malone said he was out in the Haughey residence with a friend and Ciaran came in. It was an informal hospitality morning and Mr. Haughey told Ciaran to inform Joe and his friend all about his new company. He said it was a kind of "off the-cuff remark" when it was proposed that he might like to invest in it.

On his way back from Kinsealy, his friend mentioned that it could be a good idea. He then contacted the Haugheys and told them he would like to invest. That happened in 1985 and he believed it was around 1991 or 1992 when he was again approached to invest.

Joe Malone has had a long association with Charles Haughey and Fianna Fáil. Shortly after Mr. Haughey took over the party in 1979, Joe Malone was involved in fund raising with the Friends of Fianna Fáil in the States. He and Barbara O'Neill, a first cousin of Mr. Haughey, were the main organisers.

Meat baron Seamus Purcell is another interesting investor. While leader of the opposition in late 1984, Haughey journeyed to Libya to persuade Colonel Gadaffi to buy more Irish beef. Seamus Purcell was the main beneficiary of this trip, which allowed the Tipperary cattle dealer exclusive rights to export live cattle to Libya.

The late P.V. Doyle and Charles Haughey had been close business friends for many years. Charles Haughey inaugurated the Fianna Fáil Presidential dinner shortly after he became Taoiseach in December 1979. The function is held in the Burlington Hotel, one of the Doyle family hotels. It is worth an estimated £100,000 a year to the Doyle group. Fianna Fáil uses a suite in the Berkeley Court for its fund raising operations. While Taoiseach, Charles Haughey also had the use of a suite in the hotel.

For five years, Celtic Helicopters provided Ciaran Haughey and John Barnacle with a living. But then it began receiving more money – around £300,000 – to pay off debts. A number of people passed large sums of money to Charlie Haughey's accountant, Des Traynor.

These included people who have long been associated with Haughey such as Kerry-born property developer, John Byrne. But they also included people who seemed to have no connection with Haughey – like Guy Snowden, whose company, G-Tech, made substantial money out of installing the Lotto computer system in Ireland. In 1993, shortly after he put $100,000 into Celtic, the multi-million pound Lotto contract was renewed. In 1998, Mr. Snowdon resigned from Camelot, the UK lottery operator, after he lost out in a libel case in which tycoon Richard Branson had accused Mr. Snowden of offering him a bribe in 1993 to entice him to withdraw a rival bid for the UK lottery. After the case the US businessman stood down as a director of G-Tech and sold most of his shareholding.

Another contributor was Mike Murphy, an insurance broker. He invested £100,000 but claimed it was for a man called David Gresty, from Monaco. Murphy's close business association with beef tycoon Larry Goodman was one of the things mentioned by Des O'Malley during a Dail debate on Haughey's stewardship while Taoiseach. The Tribunal heard that Mr. Murphy sent a cheque for £100,000 to Credit Suisse Bank in London with instructions that it should be lodged to an Ansbacher account. Mr. Murphy, who is also the insurance broker for Celtic Helicopters, said he believed he was told to send the cheque to this account by Paul Carty, the Irish Helicopters company accountant. He revealed that in late summer of 1992 he was approached by John Barnacle, the managing director of Celtic to see if he could find investors. He agreed to make some inquiries and found one – David Gresty of DB Agencies in Monaco who was prepared to invest £100,000 for 8 per cent of the company.

In the late 1980s, Murphy was hired by Larry Goodman to

insure beef exports to Iraq. In 1989, Murphy became Celtic's insurance broker. In April 1990, he tendered successfully to insure the Department of Agriculture's intervention beef. His bid was the lowest, so the department was obliged to accept it.

In the Dáil, Des O'Malley, who has closely scrutinised the operations of beef baron Larry Goodman over the years, pointed out the potential significance of the relationship between Murphy and Goodman.

In his evidence to the Tribunal, Ciaran Haughey revealed that he never directly or indirectly sought investment in the company by Dr. O'Connell and had not been aware he had made an investment. Nor was he aware that one of the shareholders who invested was a Mars nominee and that this company held shares in trust for various parties.

He said that he first heard of the Dr. John O'Connell investment when he received a letter as company secretary from Dr. O'Connell's solicitors. He discussed the matter with his father who said he would look into it, so he left it at that. He heard nothing more and the former Taoiseach did not tell him what passed between him and Dr. O'Connell.

Mr. Haughey said that he and Mr. Barnacle requested Des Traynor to help them raise capital for Celtic Helicopters and he agreed. Mr. Traynor raised £290,329 from five investors – Kerry businessman Xavier McAuliffe, the late Pat Butler of Butler Engineering, Portarlington, property developer John Byrne, and from Michael Murphy and Guy Snowden. He said he knew John Byrne as a friend of the family who was also a keen aviation person. He had no idea how Mr. Guy Snowden had come into the picture and was just informed he was an investor. Des Traynor had told him Murphy's investment was £100,000 but he had no knowledge of Carlisle Trust or that Mr. Murphy was connected with it.

The Tribunal was told that Mr. McAuliffe had invested £52,500 sterling in Celtic Helicopters in 1992. The Haughey family used the grounds of Mr. McAuliffe's Skellig Hotel in Dingle, Co. Kerry, as a departure point for helicopter flights to Inishvickillane. Mr. McAuliffe was appointed a director of the State-owned Great Southern Hotel group. Property developer John Byrne invested £47,532.82p in Celtic and Mr. Butler gave

£25,000. There was a $100,000 investment from Mr. Snowden and £100,000 from Michael Murphy.

John Byrne has been a major property developer for some 40 years. A site he owned in Dublin and another in Tralee benefited in 1988 and 1990 respectively when they were granted urban renewal designation. Mr. Haughey was Taoiseach and Mr. Padraig Flynn was the Minister for the Environment at the time. A third site owned by Mr. Byrne – on the east side of Parnell Square in Dublin – also received urban renewal designation in 1994. The designations gave attractive tax incentives to development on these sites.

Ciaran began his working life as an apprentice plumber with the Jones group, then run by Gerry Jones who had stood solidly behind Mr. Haughey during the Arms Crisis. After a helicopter course in Canada, Ciaran was ready to take off with a new venture in 1985. He linked up with John Barnacle, a pilot who had flown missions in Vietnam. They had the expertise, but no money, so naturally they turned to Charlie Haughey's financial wizard – the late Des Traynor.

Traynor, an accountant, was on the board of Aer Lingus and on a committee that supervised the affairs of the airline's subsidiaries, including Irish Helicopters. Traynor helped Celtic get an £80,000 loan from his bank, Guinness & Mahon. The bank was told that Irish Helicopters was effectively going to supply its rival by selling it an aircraft. The new company needed another £80,000 to buy this first helicopter. Between them, Haughey junior and Barnacle put up only £120 for which they got 60pc of the shares in Celtic. John Barnacle, managing director of Celtic Helicopters, in his evidence to the Tribunal, said he had not been aware in 1985 or at any time of Dr. John O'Connell's shareholding of £5,000. The first time he heard about it was in a letter from O'Connell's solicitors on March 5, 1992, which he passed to the company secretary – Ciaran Haughey.

Asked how much he and Ciaran Haughey were putting up while looking for a loan of £80,000 from the bank and getting another £80,000 from investors, Mr. Barnacle replied £60 each. He agreed the amount they were putting in was minimal in money terms, but the bank and others were investing in them and taking 40pc in return.

And the Tribunal learned that Charles Haughey may have been the beneficiary of another £100,000 previously untracked. The money, which was intended as an investment in Celtic Helicopters, ended up in a sterling account used to pay Mr. Haughey's bills.

Tribunal Counsel John Coughlan said there was evidence the £100,000 cheque from Michael Murphy went through Credit Suisse in London to an Ansbacher account in Zurich and then made its way back to Dublin.

He said it appeared to have ended up in the sterling S-8 account in Irish Intercontinental Bank, an account which the Tribunal already heard was used to pay the former Taoiseach's domestic bills.

Up to 1990, Celtic Helicopters was a viable company, making sufficient profit to give its two founding directors, Ciaran Haughey and John Barnacle, a livelihood. But when they decided to expand into helicopter maintenance and the provision of a hangar in 1991, debts began to mount. Celtic has since sold its hangar.

Company accountant Paul Carty outlined two 1992 meetings he had with the company's insurance broker, Michael Murphy. The first was to set out the financial position but he recalled that at the second meeting there was mention of a French colleague of Mr. Murphy's being an investor. Mr. Murphy had asked that his investment be readily identifiable in the company but Mr. Carty said he did not make much out of this request at the time and did not know why. He believed he had a phone call after the second meeting from Mr. Murphy in relation to the destination of his investment. He could not say why the amount was simply not made out to the nominee company, Overseas Nominees.

He believed the late Des Traynor was gathering the funds and they were going into an account in one lot. Mr. Carty said Mr. Traynor had given him an account number for Credit Suisse that he believed was the number of Overseas Nominees.

Mr. Carty, who was also a former non-executive director of the helicopter company, said Mr. Traynor spoke to him early in 1994 and said the company could still not command a premium. He advised that investors should be given 7 p.c. preferential shares which would be held by Larchfield Securities. In March

1996, the directors said they did not wish to identify Larchfield Securities – the Haughey family trust – as the holder of further blocks of shares. For that reason, it was to be held in the Larchfield Securities' nominated company, MIS nominees.

In early 1992, Celtic Helicopters was looking for up to £600,000 to expand its operation and meet the debt it had built up with the building of the hangar. Mr. Traynor introduced five investors between November 1992 and February 1993 – with an injection of approximately £300,000. That move was designed to enhance the balance sheet of Celtic so that it could secure a loan from Smurfit Finance.

The Tribunal also heard details about Larchfield Securities, the Haughey family trust which had a shareholding in Celtic Helicopters. The company did not trade, have a bank account or cheque book. Any funds came through Charles Haughey.

Company accountant, Ciaran Ryan, detailed its structure in a memorandum he made out following a meeting with members of the Tribunal. The directors and shareholders had given him instructions to co-operate fully. He said he was appointed in 1997 and prepared returns in order to bring company affairs up to date for the inspector of taxes.

Mr. Ryan said the company first earned income in 1996 through the letting of property at Kilmuckridge, Co. Wexford. The company was established in late 1973 and became a limited company in December 1994. Mr. Ryan told the Tribunal that the assets of the company were land and a house at Kilmuckridge; Inishvickillane, the island off the coast of Kerry; a cottage and land in Sligo; the Haughey yacht *Celtic Mist* and shares in Celtic Helicopters.

He said the cost of the initial land and construction was regarded as gifts from Charles Haughey to his four children. Mr. Charles Haughey told him that funds used for Larchfield should be put down to him personally.

The Tribunal also heard that a cheque for £10,000 from bloodstock breeder and former senator John Magnier to the then chairman of Aer Lingus, Dr. Michael Dargan, ended up forming part of the start-up capital of Celtic Helicopters. John Magnier has since stated that he was not an investor in Celtic Helicopters and had no idea that the cheque he wrote to Dr. Dargan would end up where it did. Counsel for the Moriarty Tribunal stressed that the cheque to Dr. Dargan appeared to have been "a completely legitimate payment arising out of nomination fees". It was one of six cheques that Dr. Dargan placed with Guinness & Mahon bank between January and March 1985. The six cheques ended up in an account in the name of Amiens Securities, controlled by the late Des Traynor. Mr. Traynor and Dr. Dargan were personal friends and professional associates. Dr. Dargan was chairman of Cement Roadstone Holdings from 1973 to 1987 while Mr. Traynor was a non-executive director of the same company from 1970 to 1987, when he succeeded Dr. Dargan as chairman. Apparently, it was Mr. Traynor who ensured the £10,000 went to Celtic Helicopters. "I offered no such instructions," said Dr. Dargan.

John Magnier, a close personal friend of the former Taoiseach, has been dragged into political controversy before. The Magnier Family Trusts were a beneficial shareholder of United Property Holdings (UPH), a company at the centre of controversial dealings surrounding Telecom Eireann's purchase of its headquarters site in Ballsbridge, Dublin, in 1990. Mr. Dermot Desmond, another close friend of Mr. Haughey, set up UPH. Business tycoon Dr. Michael Smurfit was among the shareholders and was also chairman of the semi-state company, Telecom Eireann. UPH was established in 1988 and bought the former Johnston Mooney and O'Brien bakery site for £4m. in November of the same year. Nine months later UPH sold it at a profit of £2m. to a complex consortium of offshore companies which, in 1991, sold it to Telecom Eireann for £9.4m.

Mr. John Glackin, a High Court inspector appointed to investigate the affair, later concluded that Mr. Desmond controlled these offshore companies and was "financially interested in them". Dr. Smurfit later resigned as Chairman of Telecom.

Mr. Desmond, who subsequently resigned as chairman of the semi-state company, Aer Rianta, found himself involved in a controversy surrounding Celtic Helicopters in 1991. Documentation prepared by Mr. Desmond's stockbroking firm NCB got into the hands of Celtic Helicopters. It had been sent to Celtic's rivals, the Aer Lingus subsidiary Irish Helicopters. Later,

Aer Lingus said it accepted at the time that Mr. Desmond had no personal knowledge of or involvement in the affair. At this time, Des Traynor was not only a member of the Aer Lingus board but was also chairman of the board's sub-committee dealing with subsidiary companies, including Irish Helicopters. He held this position from 1982 to 1992. He was in effect the single most important board member overseeing the running of the Aer Lingus subsidiary, Irish Helicopters while at the same time he was actively raising substantial funds for its main rival, Celtic Helicopters.

John Magnier, who was appointed a Senator by Charles Haughey, was also a beneficiary of the investment in Ireland by Sheikh Khalid Bin Mahfouz. The Sheikh and 10 associates and family members were granted Irish passports in 1990 in return for a promised £20 million investment. The then minister for justice, Ray Burke, signed the naturalisation certificates in his own home and the then Taoiseach, Charles Haughey, personally handed over the passports at a function in the Shelbourne Hotel. The destination of £17m. out of the £20m. investment is known. Some £4m. went to Leisure Holdings, a company which started life in 1988 as Leading Sires with the purpose of investing in bloodstock. The company's major interest at the time was making investments in Britain. The largest single shareholder was John Magnier, while the chairman was Kerry group chief executive, Denis Brosnan. In 1990, it changed its name to Leisure Holdings. In 1992, Leisure Holdings took over Classic Thoroughbreds, of which Dr. Smurfit and Mr. Desmond had been directors. Mr. J.P. McManus, a wealthy businessman mainly associated with the horse racing industry, also joined the board of Leisure Holdings. In 1993, Mr. McManus was identified by a Government inspector as a key figure in the deals surrounding the Telecom site, as his account in a Jersey bank part-funded and then profited from the series of deals leading up to Telecom's purchase of the site.

£3m. went to Kerry Airport, a project also chaired by Mr. Brosnan. Among other beneficiaries of the Mahfouz investment were businesses in which Mr. Pat Butler and Mr. Xavier McAuliffe were involved. Both men subsequently invested in Celtic Helicopters. Mr. McAuliffe was a minor shareholder in

Kerry Airport, which got Mahfouz money. A further £3m is believed to have been invested in Butler Engineering, a company of the late Pat Butler.

In 1985 Des Traynor sourced £80,000 from several investors including Mr. Cruse W Moss. Mr. Moss took out a shareholding in Celtic Helicopters in June 1985. General Automotive Corporation of which he was chairman, benefited from a major contract with CIE to build £50m worth of Bombardier buses.

And there is a further co-incidence. Joe Malone, whose son contributed £15,000 to Celtic, worked for General Automotive from 1983 to 1988, becoming executive president and president of GAC International.

11

TAXMEN
BUNGLED £2m
HAUGHEY CLAIM

When it was disclosed that a tax assessment of about £2m. against Charles Haughey was reduced to zero by an Appeals Commissioner of the Revenue Commissioners, it was as if an exocet missile had been fired into government buildings. And when it was discovered that the Commissioner involved was a brother-in-law of the Taoiseach, Bertie Ahern, the fall-out caused a major crisis for the Fianna Fáil-Progressive Democrats administration.

The issue led to a bitter debate in the Dáil just before the Christmas recess in 1988. It was the flamboyant Democratic Left TD, Pat Rabbitte who disclosed to parliament that the Appeals Commissioner who made the controversial decision was Ronan Kelly, a brother-in-law of Bertie Ahern who appointed him while Minister for Finance in 1992. Ahern made the recommendation to Government at that time without telling Taoiseach Albert Reynolds or members of the Cabinet that Kelly was his brother-in-law. Even Mr. Ahern's Government colleagues were surprised by the revelation because he never told them of his relationship with Ronan Kelly.

When he got an opportunity to raise the matter in the Dail, Deputy Rabbitte asked Mr. Ahern if he would agree that it gave the wrong impression to the public that the brother-in-law of the Leader of Fianna Fáil should adjudicate on the tax affairs of a former Leader of Fianna Fáil.

Beyond confirming that Ronan Kelly was his brother-in-law,

the Taoiseach did not respond to the question. He told the house that the first time he knew his brother-in-law had anything to do with this matter was when he read it in the morning newspapers.

After negotiations between the whips of the various parties, the Government agreed to a debate on the controversy.

Fine Gael finance spokesman, Michael Noonan, a former Minister for Justice, said that he had never experienced such outrage among taxpayers in 25 years of public life. He continued: "Their outrage is matched only by their cynicism that the system has failed them, that it does not work in a fair and just manner and that there is one law for ordinary taxpayers and another for the well heeled and influential."

He quoted from the Judge McCracken report which said that he was "satisfied beyond all reasonable doubt that all of the moneys paid by Mr. Ben Dunne were received by or on behalf of Mr. Charles Haughey for his benefit or, in one case, for the benefit of a member of his family."

Mr. Noonan said "Anybody who has even scanned the McCracken Report should not be surprised at this conclusion as Mr. Ben Dunne had in sworn evidence said he gave £1.5m to Mr. Haughey, and Mr. Haughey in his last appearance before the Tribunal admitted this was so, that he had received the money and that it was for his personal benefit."

He said the central figure in this "debacle" was not Mr. Kelly but Mr. Haughey.

He then quoted from an article by political writer Bruce Arnold in the *Irish Independent:* 'The recent revelations about his (Charles Haughey) receipt of large sums of money have inextricably linked together his exercise of power, his by-passing of constitutional requirements, his arrogant interference on a wide range of financially sensitive deals on property, on beef, on passports, on unspecified favours which earned handsome cash presents with his occupation of the highest political office.

"This by definition is corrupt. It was seen as such and challenged as such by intrepid politicians from within his own party, led by men like George Colley and Deputy Des O'Malley, and their fate like that of other lesser names, was confrontation and isolation. The rest of the Fianna Fáil Party, the vast majority, watched and did nothing. They saw the abuse of power. They saw the acquisition of gross unexplained and unjustifiable wealth. And they simulated incomprehension, bewilderment, ignorance, amnesia, stupidity.

"They were intelligent, in some cases, gifted men and women. Yet through their inertia, they subscribed to a constitutional nonsense, to a leader of their party, of successive Governments and of the country over long periods of office, acting against the country's interest and increasingly in his own personal interest. Several are in power at this moment, including the Taoiseach who enjoyed an extremely close and intimate association from the time he as Assistant Chief Whip of Fianna Fáil to his enjoyment of the powerful position of Minister for Finance.'

Mr. Noonan concluded: "Despite his attempts in recent years to distance himself from the Haughey era, this debacle has again reminded the public that the Taoiseach, for much of his political career, was Mr. Haughey's closest lieutenant. No amount of spin doctoring will erase this fact from the public consciousness."

Fine Gael leader, John Bruton told the house that the sense of outrage in the country was of "immense proportions". The idea that a former Taoiseach shamelessly frustrated a Tribunal, shamelessly told lies to a Tribunal and shamelessly abused the law to evade tax liability was causing outrage.

He continued: "The outrage is deepened by the fact that there has never been the slightest hint of contrition. There has never been the slightest demand for contrition from Mr. Haughey coming from the party that he led. There had never been a demand from Fianna Fáil, which gave so much to Mr. Haughey and reposed so much trust in him, for a genuine heartfelt apology for the way in which he conducted himself over so many years. It is time now for Fianna Fáil, which contains many honourable people who would never dream of doing anything of the kind Mr. Haughey did, to rise up and ask this man to say he is sorry for the appalling things he did and for the way in which he misled this country and demeaned our profession."

Labour Leader Ruairi Quinn had a couple of patriot missiles lined up for the Taoiseach. He began: "There is an old maxim; justice not only needs to be done but must be seen to be done. Make no mistake; nobody among the wider public believes that justice has been done in this case. A former leader of the Fianna

Fáil Party, a former Taoiseach, a patron, a mentor is making a fool of the institutions of the State and of the people he once claimed to serve, with the active support of his party, by its silence. He will not like to hear this but it is the truth; Jack Lynch once said he would not stand idly by. That is precisely what the Taoiseach and others did for more than a decade."

Warming to his theme, he went on: "During all his visits to Kinsealy, did the Taoiseach ever ask where Mr. Haughey's wealth, all that unexplained fortune, came from? Will he continue to stand idly by as he did when others, including the Tanaiste and Deputy Des O'Malley, asked the same questions? The public want to know if he will hold Mr. Haughey to account. Will he ever be held to account or is the blasé approach displayed by the Minister for Finance to continue?"

Ruairi Quinn was called a "hypocrite" by Fianna Fáil Minister of State, Noel Tracy when he fumed: "Fianna Fáil and its political culture are destroying politics in Ireland."

The Labour leader felt that the Taoiseach had a number of questions to answer, not just to the House but to the public. He went on: "Does he believe it is appropriate that his brother-in-law appointed by him, should sit in judgement on his former mentor, Charles Haughey? Does he believe that Mr. Kelly, notwithstanding his competency, should have stepped aside so that justice could not only be done but be seen to be done?"

Damage had been done, he felt, to the most valuable yet fragile of commodities, namely trust in politics and trust in our political institutions. He said the Taoiseach could not undo that damage but he could begin to repair it. He should publish the decision in respect of the Haughey case, discover who was responsible for this mess and vindicate the people's right to know.

He concluded: "The people want and deserve to know what happened in this case. If the Taoiseach comprehends the trust they have placed in him, he should discover the truth on their behalf. The bottom line is that no one, no former Taoiseach or Leader of Fianna Fáil, should be above the law."

The colourful Labour TD for Dublin South West, Pat Rabbitte (he was a member of Democratic Left before the merger with Labour) produced a couple of verbal nuggets. Some of his gems:-

"We now have a brother-in-law sitting in a quasi judicial capacity who decided to exonerate the man who played ducks and drakes with us in this House and is now doing it outside.

"When Mr. Haughey paraded his retinue like an Arab Sheikh for many years the Revenue Commissioners did not see anything wrong with it. It did not occur to them that they should ask questions.

"After parading his great wealth for years the old boss is finally caught, but with one bound he is free. This has to be explained to the people who pay their taxes as best they can. It is unconscionable that something like this could come about."

The Green Party TD, John Gormley, a former Lord Mayor of Dublin, attacked the Taoiseach's link with Mr. Haughey. "Despite all his talk about honesty and integrity, the Taoiseach has not severed the link with Mr. Haughey. He is umbilically tied to Mr. Haughey and that umbilical cord will strangle him and his Government if he does not act decisively."

He concluded: "I ask the Taoiseach to close all loopholes pertaining to Tribunals and insist that the reasons for this bizarre Appeal Commissioner's decision be published. The Taoiseach should not underestimate public anger. He is driving into GUBU land and he is at the wheel. He can decode which way to go but he and his Government are indecisive on this matter. If the Taoiseach wishes to restore public confidence in the body politic he must act decisively, distance himself from Mr. Haughey and condemn his actions."

Dublin socialist, Joe Higgins, who represents Dublin West, painted a picture of two Irelands. In one, Dublin householders were dragged in front of the Dublin District Court facing threats of entry into Stubbs Gazette, seizure of goods by a sheriff, steep court costs and judgements registered against their mortgages, "because they owe £210 arrears of an unjust and discredited water tax, now abolished, which they have objected to paying". A very sick heroin addict was sent to prison for six years for stealing a handbag. A Galway man is serving two weeks in prison for putting up posters.

"In the other Ireland, powerful bankers who facilitated tax evasion systematically over ten years have yet to darken the doorway of a courthouse. Will they ever? A former leader of

Fianna Fáil, former Taoiseach and millionaire property owner who, following a Tribunal of Inquiry which found he had evaded substantial amounts of tax, is judged to owe nothing.

"The Ireland of the golden circle used, abused and sucked dry, the Ireland of the majority of tax compliant citizens, especially PAYE workers, and now walks away scot-free. It is high time our people called an end to this and pulled down the corrupt edifice."

The Fianna Fáil benches were almost full as the Taoiseach, Bertie Ahern rose to speak. He first gave an assurance to the house: "Equity in the tax system is one of the foundations of a fair society and the Government and I are totally committed to it."

Attacking the opposition, he rejected the insinuation that the Appeal Commissioner involved "who is not particularly close to me" acted with anything less than total professional integrity or competence in this matter. To the best of his knowledge, he is not a member of Fianna Fáil, never was and never worked for the party or any other political party. He continued: "It is deeply unfair that an honourable public servant should be attacked without any opportunity for self defence and that the privileges of this House should be abused as they have been in recent days. If Deputies believe there has been a lapse of standards in the conduct of this case at any level by the relevant authorities, they are profoundly mistaken."

The Fianna Fáil leader revealed that he had "no insight" into the details of the case or the decision. But he imagined that when the Revenue Commissioners lost any particular stage in an appeal process they would do all they could to fill in any gaps or repair any weaknesses in their case before it reached the next stage.

In his brief contribution, Mr. Ahern did not answer any of the questions raised by the opposition. But he reassured "every member of the public" that there had been no breach in the integrity of public administration, which due process would continue to its ultimate conclusions and that illegal tax evasion would not go unpunished, as long as he was Taoiseach.

The Minister for Finance, Charlie McCreevy, who tried to have Haughey ousted with a no confidence motion in 1982, made it clear that he regarded tax evasion as abhorrent. The issue of an individual's tax affairs was a matter for the Revenue Commissioners. The Minister for Finance did not get involved in the question of tax liability. The appeals system was there for all taxpayers to use. The Appeals Commissioners were independent in the exercise of their duty. The then Minister for Finance (Bertie Ahern) appointed the current Commissioners validly within the law in December 1992.

He concluded: "The publicity surrounding this case suggests that the decision of an Appeals Commissioner is final. That is not the case. It is only the first stage in a process."

The Government won the ensuing vote by a majority of five, 74-69, getting support from four independents – Harry Blaney (Donegal North East), Mildred Fox (Wicklow), Thomas Gildea (Donegal West) and Jackie Healy-Rae (Kerry South).

12

A COMPLEX CHARACTER: RUTHLESS BUT CARING

Manipulative, cunning, devious, astute, autocratic, brilliant, tenacious, ruthless, lecherous, witty, articulate, charismatic, extremely generous and caring – such is the cauldron of traits that make up the colourful Haughey character.

His generosity was known particularly in his own sprawling constituency of Dublin North Central, made up mostly of a working class population, with pockets of unemployed as bad as can be found anywhere in the country. A typical gesture came at Christmas time. The manager of a local supermarket was requested to hand out 50 hampers to the most needy. Haughey paid the bill and told the manager not to mention his name in connection with the gift.

While canvassing during an election campaign, he noticed that an old lady living alone needed her fireplace fixed. The fireplace was repaired and next day she got a delivery of a ton of coal! In another case, a lady had a serious legal problem. Haughey sent a lawyer to give her advice and again paid the bill. When he attended the funeral in Tipperary of the father of his Northern Ireland advisor, Dr. Martin Mansergh, a youngster knocked at the window of his State car to say hello. CJ rolled down the window, smiled and handed the boy a £5 note. He meticulously looked after his constituents in Dublin North Central. For any death or accident, the family concerned was the recipient of a bouquet of flowers. A family in Donnycarney had all their furniture and carpets destroyed in a fire. CJ instructed his secretary, Catherine, to have the house re-furnished.

His survival through four leadership heaves is a testimony to his astuteness. The wily politician was regarded as the most professional in Leinster House since Eamon de Valera, former President, Taoiseach and founder of Fianna Fáil. His strategy was extremely clever, how to exert pressure to win the doubtful voter. Either he got somebody in authority to phone the Deputy in question and exert that pressure, or he would personally confront the TD. Both methods were invariably successful. The most notable leadership challenge was in 1983 when the dissidents' moment seemed to have come at last. His Tanaiste, Ray MacSharry, had been bugging conversations with former Cabinet colleague, Dr. Martin O'Donoghue. And there were revelations that his Minister for Justice, Sean Doherty, had been tapping journalists' phones. There were also disquieting reports from County Roscommon, that the Justice Minister was running his constituency like an old-style wild-west sheriff.

In January of that year, many of his hitherto faithful supporters including senior minister Albert Reynolds, told Haughey he must go. A substantial number of the national executive, the ruling body of the party, also expressed a view that he should step down because the people in the constituencies were turning against him. Haughey sensed that as far as he was concerned, the game was up, but informed his parliamentary party: "If I go, the decision to go will be taken in my own time."

Former Dublin Lord Mayor and only Jewish member of the Dáil Ben Briscoe put down a motion of "no confidence" in Haughey in February 1983. He became worried after a disturbing call. The situation became so ugly that Briscoe was advised by a colleague, Des O'Malley, and also by Assistant Garda Commissioner John Fleming, that he should accept a police escort until the vote was taken. At home, Ben, his wife, Carol and family fielded abusive phone calls, some of them expressing in no uncertain terms that it was a pity that Hitler had not "finished the job".

On the day of the vote, a Garda car escorted Ben Briscoe from his bungalow home in Celbridge, Co. Kildare, to Leinster House. But when he got there the Chairman of the parliamentary party, Jim Tunney – a loyal supporter of Haughey – surprised the members by adjourning the meeting because of the sudden death of Donegal TD Clem Coughlan, who incidentally had been opposed to Haughey. The ten-day adjournment gave Haughey and his loyal lieutenants, Ray MacSharry, Padraig Flynn and Paudge Brennan, some badly needed breathing space to try and recover the situation. They had persuaded Haughey to stay and fight. Forty-one TDs – a majority – had signed a petition calling for a party meeting to discuss Haughey's leadership. Haughey and his team managed to convince at least eight of them to change their minds in the intervening period and he survived the challenge to his leadership by 40 votes to 33. In that campaign there were many "jumping heads" as Government Chief Whip Seamus Brennan once called them. All of those who changed their vote succumbed to Haughey's carefully planned campaign.

One of his most effective tactics was to infiltrate the enemy camp. There was one celebrated confrontation with a Dublin TD, who had "defected " to the O'Malley camp. "Is it true that you are working with O'Malley?" Haughey asked.

"Yes," said the TD. "I believe he is the future leader of Fianna Fáil," adding sarcastically, "I also think you are past it."

Haughey went over to a cabinet, saying: "Is that right?" A few moments later he produced a file on the Deputy and let him have a brief look at it. The man was clearly in shock after what he saw there. Haughey pressed home his advantage. "Here's what I want you to do," he said slowly. "Go back to the O'Malley camp and tell me everything that goes on." The TD had no option but to obey. The tactic did not work however, because Des O'Malley was circumspect in everything he said to the Dublin TD. Another "007" operative for Haughey was his media guru, P.J. Mara. During one heave against his leadership, Mara was asked to report on who attended the meetings of dissidents in Setanta House, across the street from Leinster House. Haughey's former Cabinet colleague, Des O'Malley, was then an independent having been forced to leave Fianna Fáil for what the National Executive, the ruling body, termed "conduct unbecoming" and was co-ordinating a putsch against his leader. He operated from a secluded office beside the Pink Elephant club in Molesworth Street. Supporters of O'Malley spotted Mara behind a car on the street. "Stand up P.J.," shouted the O'Malley supporter. Clearly embarrassed, P.J. said feebly that he was thinking of buying something for his wife Breda in the adjoining ladies' boutique! Haughey's long time companion, Terry Keane, also provided some useful information. While dining with some friends in a restaurant on the quays in Dublin, she noticed a couple of Fianna Fáil rebels having a tête-à-tête. Terry immediately phoned her "Sweetie" who was at a Cabinet meeting. Some Dáil ushers also provided useful information to Haughey during some of the heaves, providing the names of TDs and Senators who attended the O'Malley meetings.

Mr. Haughey's attention to every detail was the hallmark of his success. Before he attended any dinner function, he demanded to know who was on his right and left side and ordered brief c.v.'s on those sitting closest to him.

There are many stories of Haughey's browbeating, bullyboy tactics stretching back to the days when he was Minister for Health in the late seventies. Anybody with whom he was in regular contact was liable to get caught in his line of fire. When Minister for Health, a civil servant handed him a report. The Minister had a quick look, said it was a "load of rubbish" and in a fit of temper dumped it on the floor. He was not prepared for the Civil Servants reaction. The man coolly walked over to CJ, · caught him by the lapels of his coat and shouted: "Don't you ever do that again or I'll throw you out the fucking window!" They two men met on a daily basis. At that time CJ did not contact him for a week and apologised to him in a typical roundabout way. He mentioned something pleasant about the man's wife. The bottom line was that he had a new respect for the official for having the guts to do what he did.

He had many stormy sessions with his first Government Press Secretary, Frank Dunlop, who had also acted for his predecessor, Jack Lynch. When Dunlop arrived in the Taoiseach's office one Monday morning, Haughey was immediately confrontational.

He shouted at Dunlop: "Where the fuck were you yesterday?"

Dunlop sarcastically replied: "Yesterday was Sunday, wasn't it?"

Haughey didn't like the smart reply. He turned to the others at the meeting and said: "The bollix has a brain. He remembered it was Sunday."

As he stormed out of the meeting, Frank Dunlop shouted:

"Don't ever talk to me like that."

Mr. Haughey's genial political advisor, the late Padraig O Hanrachain ran after Frank Dunlop, saying: "You can't talk to the Taoiseach like that."

Dunlop countered: "You have it wrong, Padraig. He can't talk to me like that." They did not meet for a week, but again Haughey apologised in a roundabout way by asking Frank Dunlop, in a sheepish voice, to come up to his office.

When Minister for Justice in the sixties, he had a celebrated brush with the powerful secretary of the department, Peter Berry, a civil servant who had served with no less than fourteen Ministers for Justice during his long career. They had a minor row about an appointment. And when the young Minister for Justice did not get his way he threw the file on the floor. Berry stormed out of the office leaving it there.

Newly elected TDs Sean Power of Kildare the later Minister for Arts and Culture, Sile de Valera also incurred the wrath of their party leader by asking questions about reports in the "Backchat" column of the *Sunday Independent*. These referred to a private deal which the then Taoiseach, Charles Haughey, had negotiated with the newly elected independent Roscommon TD Tom Foxe. When they queried if the reports were true and if he could give details, CJ gave them the "Mae West" treatment. "Call up and see me in my rooms," he said casually. A couple of hours later when they arrived in his rooms, CJ tore into them. "How the fuck did you get past convention?" he asked the two bewildered TDs who were taken aback by the venom in the Taoiseach's attack.

A couple of years later, Sean Power used the Haughey attack effectively against him. In the last leadership crisis meeting in November, 1991, three months before Mr. Haughey resigned, Power, a bookmaker from Kildare and son of former Minister for Defence Paddy Power, reminded his colleagues of the "real" Haughey when he spoke at a meeting in the party rooms in Leinster House, when twenty-two deputies voted no confidence in Charles Haughey. They included Albert Reynolds who was to succeed him, European Commissioner Padraig Flynn and the former Justice Minister Maire Geoghegan'Quinn. Mr. Haughey survived until the Doherty bombshell two months later.

Dublin North East TD, Liam Fitzgerald also had some memorable clashes with his leader, including one in 1987 when CJ effectively imposed his son Sean on the Fianna Fáil organisation. The three candidates selected - the present Minister for the Marine, Dr. Michael Woods, the late Ned Brennan, and Liam Fitzgerald - had privately agreed that they would not back young Haughey, who had just completed a term as Lord Mayor of Dublin. To try and woo Fitzgerald, CJ had three meetings with him. In the first, both exchanged earthy language and CJ knew he could not change Fitzgerald's attitude. At a second meeting CJ effused charm. In his private room, the family silver was displayed as he poured on the magic words. "Your potential has never been fully realised by the party," he told Fitzgerald. But his guest refused to accept the hospitality and stood during the entire meeting. CJ resorted to barrack-room language in their third meeting again without success. Liam Fitzgerald stormed out of his office, refusing to co-operate in any way. The result was that Sean Haughey failed in his election bid. But he was successful a couple of years later when CJ resigned from his old constituency of Dublin North Central.

But the worst case of bullying from the former Taoiseach came when he clashed with three Wicklow councillors and a solicitor, who had been calling for his resignation. On a cold wintry day, all four were summoned to Kinsealy. They arrived at 8 a.m. and were not even offered a cup of tea. One by one he saw them. Three were persuaded to change their attitude but the fourth, Wicklow solicitor Sean O'Brien, refused to change his mind and repeated that Mr. Haughey should step down. O'Brien, who was in a short list for a judgeship, came out of the meeting ashen faced. "I am dead; I am finished," he told colleagues after his bitter exchange with party leader. Shortly after this meeting, Sean O'Brien, totally disillusioned with Haughey's autocratic style, emigrated to Australia with his wife and four young children.

The late Joe Moore, boss of the PMPA, was used on three occasions to put pressure on people to support Haughey. One of these was the late Tim Killeen, who worked for McKearns Motors, a subsidiary of the PMPA. When the current Foreign Minister, David Andrews, a practising barrister known to be opposed to Haughey's leadership, lost his PMPA work, he stormed into Haughey's office and demanded to have it restored or he would "blow it" to the newspapers. The PMPA brief was restored to David Andrews within a week proving that Haughey was indirectly involved.

The undermining of Government Chief Whip Seamus Brennan was another classic Haughey move. Brennan had been General Secretary of Fianna Fáil and suggested to Cork businessman Barra O Tuama that they should commission an opinion poll to see what sort of support there was for a new party. The result showed 25 per cent of voters were interested, so that Brennan was indirectly responsible for the establishment of the Progressive Democrat party. Haughey knew that Seamus Brennan was influential in the anti-Haughey camp so he removed him from all the internal Fianna Fáil committees while he was still General Secretary! Brennan had no option but to resign his post and he then campaigned successfully for a Dáil seat.

The bullying tactics used by Charles Haughey were not confined to TDs and party colleagues. He used the same tactics at Cabinet level. One Minister, Michael Woods, the current Minister for the Marine, was reduced to tears at a Government meeting. When he interjected in a discussion, Haughey shouted at him: "Who asked you to speak?" A couple of Ministers later challenged Haughey and said he should never talk to a Cabinet colleague in that fashion.

In the Ministerial corridor behind Leinster House one afternoon, Mr. Haughey was obviously bored. So he decided to have some fun. Over one of the doors was the name, Ray MacSharry, Minister for Finance. The Taoiseach had enormous respect for his Minister. He walked past the office. Over the next door was the name of the Minister for Agriculture, Michael O'Kennedy, who also carried the powerful title of trustee of Fianna Fáil and was the only Cabinet Minister in the outgoing Lynch government to vote for Haughey. Mr. Haughey, apparently, did not have respect for his Minister. The Taoiseach was seen by an usher to kick the door and shout: "What are you up to O'Kennedy?"

One of his closest political friends was the late Brian Lenihan who, despite his formidable intellect, was completely dominated by the Taoiseach. In 1982 when Haughey and Lenihan attempted to move the formidable Sean Donlon from his post as Irish Ambassador to Washington, Brian Lenihan agreed to give me an off-the-record briefing. He greeted me in his office in Iveagh House and I assured him at the beginning that the meeting was completely off the record and none of what he said would be attributable to him. For fifteen minutes, Brian Lenihan talked around the story without giving me any new information. In the middle of the meeting, he repeated: "This is off the record". I assured him it was. As he finished the meeting, having giving me nothing, I again assured him that the meeting was off the record. I was half way across Stephen's Green, on my way to Leinster House, when I heard somebody shouting "Kevin, Kevin". I looked around. It was the Foreign Minister, out of breath. All he said was: "That was off the record".

And there were clashes with former President Mary Robinson on a number of issues but mainly about the limits of her role while she was the occupant of Aras an Uachtarain. The former Senator and lawyer (and later United Nations representative on human rights) had promised to push out new frontiers during her presidency. But Haughey, who saw himself as the real President of Ireland, attempted to limit her powers at every opportunity. He prevented her on occasions from doing interviews and curbed her travels abroad to give speeches. When she sought permission to do certain things, Haughey's response to many of her requests was: "It is not appropriate".

Journalists were very much in his line of fire. At a briefing for political correspondents in New York, it was noticeable that the vibes were bad between Mr. Haughey and the then political correspondent of the *Irish Times*, Dick Walsh. Haughey pointedly asked Walsh why he never addressed him as Taoiseach. "Have you no respect for the office?" he asked. Walsh's reply was a classic. "It is because I do have respect for the office of Taoiseach that I call you Mr. Haughey."

When confronted by an *Irish Independent* journalist at the Berkeley Court Hotel to comment on the latest I.M.S. opinion poll, which was extremely critical of his leadership and of the Fianna Fáil party, he had three short colourful comments to make. He told the *Irish Independent's* political reporter, Mairtin

MacCormaic: "Fuck you, fuck the I.M.S. and fuck the *Irish Independent!*"

13

WERE YOU CHARLES HAUGHEY'S MISTRESS?

While Terry Keane wrote about her relationship with CJ many times in her popular column, *The Keane Edge* on the back page of the *Sunday Independent*, she seldom spoke in public about it. But she did call the Radio Ireland lunchtime show one Sunday after a piece in the *Sunday Tribune*. Terry admitted to being a "close friend" of Mr. Haughey and added: "I still am a close friend." She told interviewer John Ryan: "Close friends don't let each other down or walk away when tragedy strikes the other." She described the media stories on CJ Haughey at the time as a "witch-hunt" and said the public was suffering from "national amnesia" when they spoke about his finances.

Terry told the nation: "When we talk to-day about the so-called Celtic Tiger economy, we forget those dark days when we were literally running out of credit. We needed someone to put a sophisticated and stylish image and restore confidence in the country. I think that Mr. Haughey probably was the man that did that." Asked if she ever had any questions of her own on how he got his money, Terry replied: "I never discussed those sort of matters with him. I am as shocked and as saddened as everybody else about the events that have unravelled. But you don't walk away from somebody when something like this happens."

Pressed further by John Ryan, she was asked: "It might have occurred to you that here was this wealth and where was the income coming from?"

Her reply: "No, I didn't think about it any more than most people close to him. He has that sort of style and charisma that one takes it for granted."

And then a note of regret from Terry: "Maybe one should not have done. One doesn't ask one's close friends when they buy you a bottle of champagne where did you get the money for that. I think that is ignorant and untoward. You don't question that sort of thing."

She was then asked to describe her relationship with Charles Haughey.

"Mr. Haughey is a very good friend of mine and a very close friend of mine. He has been one of the greatest influences on my life. He was wonderful to me in my darkest moments. And we have all had dark moments. He stood by me loyally and I think that he is much loved by many people. I think when you elevate - and let's face it, it was the people of this country which put him on a pedestal – then when he is toppled, as he has been, a lot of people feel sadness and sympathy.

"Of course, I have sympathy. I have sympathy for his family and for the man himself and for all his loved ones."

John Ryan then came to the crunch question. "You have been described as Charlie Haughey's mistress. Do you think that is a fair description?"

Her reply was a classic. "I think they should call the Keane Edge maybe Mr. Haughey's mistress."

Journalist Sam Smyth touched on her favourite city – Paris – in the hope of teasing out a gem. But he was out-foxed by the *Sunday Independent* gossip writer. Said Sam: "You are supposed to be sharing Paris as your favourite city with Charlie Haughey." Her reply: "Is Paris one of your favourite cities?"

Smyth asked her if women found Haughey attractive, as he obviously found them. Terry's reply: "I think that he was a man of great charisma. I think that when he walked into a room everybody noticed him - men and women. I think that is the charm of the man. And rich and poor were attracted by him, and powerful people and not so powerful people.

"I think Charlie was unusual in the sense of an Irishman – he does like women. He does enjoy their company. So many Irishmen are interested in women in the bed. But they don't really want to talk to them or spend time with them."

In her column in the *Sunday Independent* there were many teasers, laced with innuendo and clever word play. She portrayed herself as having some form of unique and special relationship with Charles Haughey.

In an account of a champagne reception in the week that Haughey was finally ousted from power in February 1992, she quoted a French aristocrat as pointing out that "even in France a few eyebrows were raised when the President appointed his ex-mistress as premier. Never in the history of France had anything quite so outrageous as that happened." And then the usual teaser: "Nor in this country ... so where did I go wrong?"

Beneath a picture of Charles Haughey, Terry wrote: "Throughout the night my phone hopped to the common theme 'what will Charlie do now? What will he do now! Now that Charlie has given up the day job, infinite vistas open up for the enjoyment of life. Venice in February was a delight he savoured all too rarely while the clammy hand of the Fianna Fáil parliamentary party stayed him. Early spring on the island with the deer and the antelope was a stranger to him while the Ard Fheis adulation had to be faced. The summer wine of our beloved South of France was a bouquet rather than a bottle. Fall will have a whole new meaning now. No longer the consequence of parliamentary pushing and shoving. It will be a season of trysts and mellow truthfulness. And after all that, winter will be ... content. So what will Charlie do now? The good times are only beginning."

Comparisons with his close friend, Mitterand were regular in her column. Commenting on a *Sunday Times* article on Mitterand's love life, she wrote: "Only the British would see something sinister in a prime minister having a mistress. The French know that the secret of a stable government is a stable mistress. My readers, unlike *Sunday Times* readers, have known for many a long day about Francois Mitterand's love life. He has shared many a tryst in the mist of Kerry with his petite amie Madame Guimaud, who has a holiday home there. And I've told you all before about the many times they entertained myself and my own petite ami there. Danielle Mitterand knows all about it, too, and I doubt that she has a problem with it."

A piece later on the opening of the Dingle, Co. Kerry regatta was also revealing. It read: "He stood on the prow of the Celtic Mist". She then gave a loving description of his Charvet navy blazer with the special crested gold buttons and the Charvet monogrammed shirt, his penchant for quoting Yeats at the drop of a Charvet hat. It concluded with a moving picture of Citizen Charlie sailing into the sunset to his island home.

In another audacious piece about Mr. Haughey's yacht, she wrote: "No smoking on board ship is Sweetie's rule. Indeed, mine is the only elegant plume you'll ever see emerging from the captain's cabin on board the Celtic Mist."

There were many references to their shared delights – if you could decipher them. Recalling Stephen Roche's victory in the Tour de France, she wrote: "How I remember standing at the window of my suite in the Cing watching with pride, Stephen and Charlie on the winner's rostrum, two men at the peak of their physical prowess."

She didn't mince her words in another piece headed: "Bertie's got a Terry too." She wrote: "Every Taoiseach, they say must have his Terry. And vice versa. I'm not suggesting the current Taoiseach (Bertie Ahern) could ever follow in Sweetie's footsteps – heaven, earth and all the universes forfend – but he too has his Terry. They do it behind closed doors, and even in hotel rooms. However, I can assure you the Taoiseach keeps his tie on at all times. I know because I've seen the videotapes.

"Of course, where I rendered powerful men inarticulate with lust, Terry Prone renders them the other way round, so to speak. Thus it's no surprise that Bertie is doing the honours for his Terry at a lavish lunch in Carr Communications' new headquarters today. All guests get a chance to meet the power behind the Prone. Or vice versa."

Terry wrote a funny piece on President Clinton's use of the name "Sweetie" for his well-documented trysts in the White House with his former intern, Monica Lewinsky: "I have a bone to pick (no, most emphatically not that one) with Bill Clinton. He has brought shame – there's no fancy way of saying this – on a great name. No, I'm not talking about that damp squib, if you'll pardon the expression, called that Starr report. For heaven's sake, so Clinton betrayed his wife – quelle surprise. If he was beating her it might have been impeachable, but we all know that if betraying one's wife were impeachable, scarcely one American President would have seen his term through.

"Bill Clinton didn't betray his country. In fact, he never stopped working for it, though I must admit taking calls from Congressmen while having oral sex performed on one is not the normal definition of phone sex. But I digress.

"Bill Clinton let me down. He reads this column – that's allowed. But ripping it off is another matter. And what name did he call out in passion? What love word did he reach for to soothe the breast of the loved one? "Sweetie" – that's what. Well, there's only one Sweetie, as you all know. And he's copyrighted ... to moi."

She wrote a good piece on CJs contribution to the nation, responding to critical pieces by other journalists:

"Sweetie had – and has – the vision thing. He also has imagination, passion, lust and a taste for the good things in life. In short all the things that matter at the end of the day. Sweetie is full of beans; the rest are just bean counters and has beens – indeed in some cases I doubt if they are even human beans.

"The great thing about adversity – even if it's only a minor Tribunal – is that you find out who your friends are, and believe me, Sweetie has plenty of those.

"Personally I wonder about those who complain that while he was single-handedly saving the entire economy (from '87 to '89), Sweetie didn't have the time, or the inclination, to attend to the minor details of housekeeping. Would they prefer a premier who paid his milk bill on time, to the nearest penny, but made a dog's dinner of the economy?

"By way of consolation might I point out that history is not so harsh a judge as a hungry hysterical hack on a high. There are countless politicians around the world who lined their pockets, and screwed their people. As far as the former is concerned, Sweetie wouldn't risk spoiling the line of a suit .... and as for the latter ... well suffice it to say he did the state some service."

The late comic actor Dermot Morgan referred many times to the Haughey-Keane romance in his hilarious *Scrap Saturday* radio programme. Mr. Haughey's wife, Maureen, a daughter of the late Taoiseach, Sean Lemass and mother of three sons and a daughter, did not react favourably. A discreet phone call was made to the producers to desist. Their representations proved to be unsuccessful.

There were many phone calls shared each day. CJ called Terry at 10 a.m.,2 p.m. and 7 p.m. The big question for many people who knew about regular telephone calls between them was how did she contact him at his family home in Kinsealy without being spotted by Mr. Haughey's wife, Maureen?

We can reveal how this was done. When the call was made, a special code was used: "This is Catherine, Dr. Mansergh's secretary." Dr. Mansergh was Mr. Haughey's Northern Ireland advisor.

14

GOSSIP QUEEN ADMITS 27-YEAR AFFAIR

Terry Keane shocked the nation on May 14th when she publicly admitted her 27-year affair with Charles Haughey. The wife of Supreme Court judge Ronan Keane revealed that she believed Mr. Haughey still loved her and that she loved him very much.

She also claimed that she wanted to tell her story before my book was published. *Sunday Independent* Editor, Aengus Fanning took a different view. He felt that Ms. Keane's sudden departure from his newspaper to write for the *Sunday Times* was financially motivated and not as she told Gay Byrne due to disillusionment with her column. He revealed that the *Sunday Independent* could not match the substantial package she had been offered – believed to be a six figure sum.

This is an extract from the Late Late Show interview, one of the most sensational in the 37-year history of the programme.

After being welcomed by the audience, she told Gay: "I gave him in my notice to-day to the *Sunday Independent*. It was the happiest day of my life. When I started the column it was fun. It became an instant success. It became like a monster. The more successful it became the bitchier it had to become. I became very disillusioned and I felt very guilty about it.

Two years ago I became very ill. I felt I did not want to be associated with something like that. It hurt a lot of people. When you are facing your own mortality, do I really want to be associated and be known as the woman who reveals all about everybody.

Gay – What was the nature of your illness?

Terry – I had a heart disease. For the first time in my life I started being healthy. I started walking stopped smoking on and off. I think the system was so shocked. I had to change my lifestyle. If I had died at that point, what would I be remembered for? I wouldn't be remembered for the fact that I had 4 lovely children, that these were important in my life. Because the column had alluded to my relationships with Charles Haughey: there was always some innuendo about it. All of these things – I just wanted to tell my story. I wanted to stop being associated with that column. My name was associated with it. I had to take responsibility. I am not shirking that. I wrote some of it. It is over.

I won't be writing the same type of column in the *Sunday Times*. It will be very different. It will be a current affairs. It will be comment. It will be more serious.

Gay – It will be you and not written by anybody else. And you will have more control.

Terry – Absolutely.

Gay – As you say, the *Sunday Independent* alluded again and again to Sweetie. How long was the affair with Charlie Haughey?

Terry – I met Charlie Haughey 27 years ago.

Gay – Where?

Terry – We met at a gathering. It was a dinner party in a friends house.

Gay – Was it instant attraction?

Terry – Well it was instant attraction. I didn't particularly like him before that. That often happens. You don't think about someone until you are face to face, as we were, and started talking. There was a very strong mutual attraction.

Gay – What attracted you to him?

Terry – He was very attractive and he is very attractive. He is strong, clever, entertaining, amusing, irreverent, wonderful. This is my story, let him tell his story.

Gay – What do you think attracted him?

Terry – I think he was attracted to me. We had a relationship for so long, yes. I think he loved me very much. I love him very much.

Gay – Did you ever think about running away at any stage?

Terry – No, we were both married to other people.

Gay – How long after it went on did Maureen find out?

Terry – I don't know. We never talked about each other's spouses. Charlie is an old fashioned sort of man. That would really be beyond the bounds of decency. Of course Maureen knew about it.

Gay – And she has known about it for many years?

Terry – I am sure she has, as my husband and family have.

Gay – The actual handling of the affair, safe houses and so on ...

Terry – I heard about the book that was being written by somebody else. I heard from people who had seen the script that it was a very loveless relationship, punctuated only by expensive dinners or trips on yachts. It wasn't like that. I wanted to show that it really was love. Yes people did get hurt. But you can't help who you fall in love with. Of course if we were all perfect, we wouldn't hurt anyone. But my family and his family got hurt. And I am sorry that my family and his family got hurt. We had daily contact. People talk about affairs and they think about sex. Sex is a very small part of an affair. Affairs are about trust and friendship, looking after each other and supporting each other. When one of you is in trouble, defending one ... The good times and the bad times.

Gay – But there were presumably yachts and Inishvickillane?

Terry – Absolutely.

Gay – And safe houses. You stayed in peoples houses?

Terry – It sounds as if we were on the run. No, friends that would invite us to dinner in their house, yes.

Gay – But surely you must have known that it would not remain hidden. He was the Taoiseach.

Terry – Not initially.

Gay – No of course not. But it went on after he was Taoiseach?

Terry – Yes.

Gay – That must have put an additional strain and dimension to the whole thing?

Terry – I suppose it added to it, if I am really honest. It does make it more attractive, yes, if somebody is Taoiseach.

Gay – Would he have discussed the affairs of State with you?

Terry – Yes. He would. He told many people that I had great political judgement and acumen. He would often discuss things and listen to me and change his mind slightly on things.

Gay – Were there sad times in this affair too?

Terry – There are always sad times. It was real life. It wasn't a movie. Of course, we had our bad times and good times. I am very hurt and was very hurt by the things people are saying about him now. They have forgotten all the good things he has done for this country.

Gay – Such as?

Terry – I think a lot of people to-night would not be in their jobs if it wasn't for Charlie. I think that when Ireland was a begging bowl, Charlie went out and eyeballed people in Europe and in the world. He started the Financial Services in this country, he created the Celtic Tiger. He looked after women with the Succession Act. A man could die and leave everything to the Church which they usually did in those days. He stopped that. He helped women to be secure. We know what he did for old age pensioners and the free bus passes which gave them freedom.

Gay – He was an outstanding Minister for Health.

Terry – He was. He was the very first man in the whole world to put health warnings on cigarettes. He has done amazing things. He did amazing things for artists as well. I think people forget that.

Gay – It was certainly overshadowed by what happened subsequently. Do you think now that he is being treated harshly?

Terry – I think he is treated very, very badly. I really do. I think people should see the man as a whole. Not because he didn't pay Income Tax. I don't defend what he did. But we are all flawed. Nobody is perfect. I think he did amazing things. I know his love for this country is enormous. And I know that what was said in the media is not reflected by the plain people of Ireland. He gets hundreds and thousands of letters all the time. I remember a few months ago on Prime Time, I was so revolted and disgusted by the fact that somebody stood up and said – oh we live in very interesting times, when we have for the Church, Brendan Smyth doing what he did. And in the political arena we had Charlie Haughey doing what he did. Brendan Smyth buggered little boys. Charlie has never done that. Charlie took money from people who were very willing to give it to him, so that he would have to go out and not have to worry about his own finances, so that he could run this country, which he did brilliantly and brought us the Celtic Tiger and brought us the prosperity we have to-day.

Gay – People will be ringing on the phone, Terry to say that other people took money but they had the tendency to pay tax on it now and then. *(applause)* You know all this.

Terry – Of course he should have paid taxes. I think that he has settled all that now. I am not saying that he should not pay taxes.

Gay – Did he know you were coming on the Late Late show to-night?

Terry – Yes, he did. I had lunch with him yesterday.

Gay – And he knows about this serialisation going in the *Sunday Times*.

Terry – Yes, he does.

Gay – Starting on Sunday. Did he ask you not to?

Terry – No he didn't ask me not to. I think he knows that I love him and I will be honest about our relationship. I am not saying anything that people haven't known. I think he knows that what I will say about him is a lot better than the vilification he is going through every day in the papers.

Gay – Do you still love him?

Terry – Yes, very much

Gay – Does he still love you?

Terry – I think so yes.

Gay – You can go as far as you want to on this and then stop – what about your husband? What is his reaction to all this?

Terry – I love my husband. He loves me. Maureen loves Charlie and Charlie loves Maureen. You have been here in this chair. You have seen that people don't always behave well. People may try to be good. People get hurt. It is real life. It is not some utopia where everything is perfect. My husband knows that I am writing this book. He is fully supportive of it.

Gay – One of the reasons you want to do it is to stop other people from doing their version of it.

Terry – Well it's my story. It is what happened to me. It is not just about Charlie obviously.

Gay – Do you realise that you were on the Late Late Show almost precisely 10 years ago to-day. We talked to you and your daughter Madeleine and Grace O'Shaughnessy and her daughter and Eileen Reid and her daughter. Madeleine was absolutely charming on the programme. I saw the tape the other day. It made me laugh because she described you in one word – melodramatic. She told the story of leaving home one morning to go to work and between the time she left the house and phoned you, you had a row with somebody. Madeleine rang back to the house and said: hello Mammy how are you. And you said: I am standing here at the kitchen sink. I am looking out at the garden. I am thinking about the tragedy that has been my life and I feel like a Checkov heroin. And she said – what was my Mam – melodramatic. You are a Granny and a mother of four now.

Terry – I am.

Gay – And you had lunch with Joan Collins. What did you talk about, you two?

Terry – We were both laughing about it. If anybody did hear us, they wouldn't believe it. We were both talking about our children. We felt it was very important for youngsters to get some sort of trade or profession in life. She said their families were hurt every day by the sleazy innuendo and the sleazy hack type stories. They suffer every day from what they hear in the papers. I think what I say in my story they will recognise as truth and I don't think it will hurt them.

Gay – Is there anything now you would like to do for Charlie, in his present situation?

Terry – I would like people to change and show a little more compassion to a man who actually is a very good man, who has been villified. I mean, o.k. he was wrong. He did wrong. He is not perfect. But he has done some very good things. And like everybody else he is a mixture of good and bad.

Gay – Are you sorry about the whole thing. Are you sorry that you ever got involved ... about the affair, about your life?

Terry – I am sorry about the Keane Edge, yes. I very deeply regret that.

Gay – It is only a newspaper column, you know.

Terry – I did regret that. I have to be honest and say that I don't regret the affair. Charlie was a very important part of my life. He shaped me. He changed me in many ways. We have had a wonderful time together. Yes, I am sorry, but you can't have one thing without another. I am sorry that people do get hurt. I am not a candidate for Heaven. I am just telling you my story. He must tell you his. I can't talk for him. I am sorry.

Gay – What you are saying to me is that you are no angel but neither are you that bloody awful bitch that people think you are?

Terry – I hope I am not as bad as that.

15

THE CARYSFORT
BONANZA

Few episodes illustrate Haughey's style of power better than the Carysfort saga. Indeed, so extraordinary was the way he handled the sale of this valuable piece of land in south Dublin, that it would seem to indicate a growing recklessness about the norms of government. Perhaps, given what we know now, it was also a sign of desperation. Haughey had become more and more dependent on the goodwill of rich businessmen to maintain his lavish lifestyle.

The lands around Carysfort College belonged to the nuns of the Sisters of Mercy. The lands were potentially of huge value if developed for housing, but it would not be easy to get planning permission. Nevertheless, the nuns, facing a decline in vocations and the closure of the college, were anxious to sell at a reasonable price. A group of developers - one from Northern Ireland and two from the Republic - decided to take a chance on the lands and paid £2m for the 20-acre site, a pretty keen price. Remarkably, though, the Government Valuation Office had put a value of £3.8m on the site, or £190,000 per acre. There was also practical evidence of what such a site might be worth. A nearby property in St Helen's sold in May 1989 for £7 million – seventy acres at £100,000 per acre.

This was exactly the same price the three developers paid for Carysfort, but their attempts to get planning permission failed. It appeared they had gambled heavily and lost. Then the whole affair took an unexpected turn for the better.

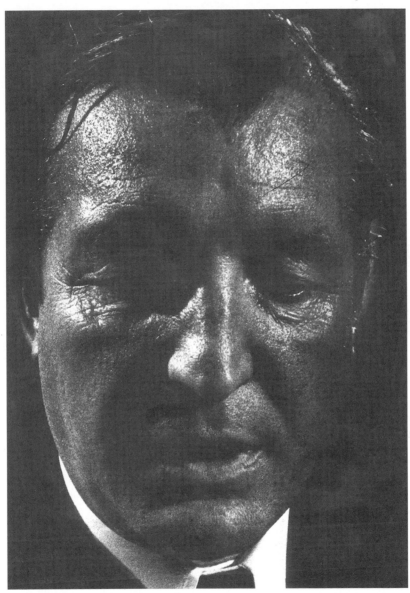

One of the most dramatic pictures ever taken of Charles Haughey, he had just been found not guilty in 1970 of importing arms into this country. The prize winning picture is by Sunday World Chief Photographer Tom McElroy. ©

The Kingdom at Kinsealy ... after their All Ireland victory, the Kerry team and their trainer Mick O'Dwyer visited Kinsealy.
Pic: Colman Doyle ©

The Kinsealy Fox meeting his old buddy the late Neil Blayney, who was also found not guilty of gun running.
Pic: Colman Doyle ©

A meeting with is "bete noire" – former Minister Des O'Malley.
Pic: Colman Doyle ©

A free man ... walking away from the arms trial in 1970, where he had been found not guilty of importing arms into this country. On his right is his solicitor the late Pat O'Connor.
Pic: Tom McElroy ©

Researcher Ann Woodfull admiring the magnificent view from the 17th floor of the Hyatt Regency Grand Cypress Hotel, where business executive Ben Dunne had his problems with the local police.

Orlando policeman Stan Spanich who arrested Ben Dunne in the Hyatt Regency Grand Cypress Hotel in Orlando, greeting the author Kevin O Connor.

Le Coq Hardi Restaurant ... where
Charlie Haughey & Terry Keane
spent at least £1,000 per week.
Pic: Donal Doherty ©

The dining room of Le Coq Hardi where Charlie and Terry dined
with intimate friends. The beautiful chandelier is seen overhead.
Pic: Donal Doherty ©

A caring Taoiseach ... With the Minister for Arts & Culture Síle de Valera, a grand-daughter of the founder of Fianna Fáil, former Taoiseach and President the late Eamon de Valera.
Pic: Colman Doyle ©

Charlie the joker ... The former Taoiseach has a wonderful sense of humour.
Pic: Tom McElroy ©

In Dublin's Fair City where Charlie boy was so pretty.
Pic: Colman Doyle ©

Wine, women and party-time ... Charlie Haughey, his mistress Terry
Keane and Terry's daughter Madeleine at the opening of a Kerry hotel.
Pic: M. Cooper Galvin

Charlie (Pavoritti) Haughey demonstrating his singing skills.
Pic: Colman Doyle ©

"Talk about the horse bolting."
Pic: Colman Doyle ©

C.J. at the Hustings.
Pic: Colman Doyle ©

Mass hysteria on the election trail.
Pic: Colman Doyle ©

C.J. at the crossroads of life reflecting on the Tribunal,
court cases and his future.

Pic: Colman Doyle ©

"We'll fight them on the beaches, we'll fight them on the shores,
land sea and air we'll fight them everywhere."

Pic: Colman Doyle ©

In happy moments ... With his predecessor Jack Lynch.
Pic: Colman Doyle ©

Charlie and Maureen in a relaxed pose
on their island.
Pic: Colman Doyle ©

C.J. the arts enthusiast.
Pic: Colman Doyle ©

The Lambay Island Sailor, going with the flow in the changeable
weather conditions.
Pic: Colman Doyle ©

Haughey tackling the
wind, lusting for life.
"Ahoy Charlie lad."
Pic: Tom McElroy ©

"Everything all right Boss"?
"Yes" Mara.
Pic: Charles Collins ©

Chatting amiably with his friend the late Brian Lenihan, while
former President Erskine Childers looks on disdainfully.
Pic: Tom McElroy ©

Haughey the island man – rugged, out in all weathers, hair tossed
to the wind with Dingle builder Dan Brick who built his island home.
Pic: Colman Doyle ©

Haughey the sailor ... Jaw set to the wind, enjoying the elements with close
friends the late Pat O'Connor, Tom Stafford and his son Conor.
Pic: Colman Doyle ©

"The Statesman" reviewing the troops.
Pic: Colman Doyle ©

C.J. Haughey meets the old IRA veterans.
Pic: Colman Doyle ©

Maggie I'm always thinking of you .....
Yes! Charlie boy.
Pic: Colman Doyle ©

The former Taoiseach in relaxed mood after receiving his seal of
office from former President Dr. Paddy Hillery.
Pic: Colman Doyle ©

Charlie stumped once again.
Pic: Colman Doyle ©

C.J. at the Dingle Regatta, shortly after the arms
trial for which he was found not guilty.
Pic: Colman Doyle ©

Brian Lenihan, presenting his warm up speech about his "fuhrer",
C.J. Haughey.
Pic: Colman Doyle ©

Charlie the bird watcher ... Admiring the bird life in his island sanctuary.
Pic: Colman Doyle

Pino Harris was a shrewd businessman who had made a fortune importing Hino trucks from Japan and selling them in Ireland and Britain. The British market was especially lucrative for him, because he could sell his imported trucks more cheaply than the English dealers. This was due to two factors, firstly because there were restrictions on direct imports into the UK and secondly because these restrictions did not apply to imports from another EU country, like Ireland. It was well known that Harris was a friend and supporter of Haughey.

Harris bought Carysfort for £6.25 million, giving the original investors a handsome profit. He had been persuaded that it was possible to turn the college into a private third level institution, attracting students from the US, the middle East and from Ireland who would pay hefty fees for tuition at an international university institution in Dublin. The idea was the brainchild of Laurence Finnegan, headmaster of the expensive fee-paying Sutton Park Secondary School. While the idea had merit, it quickly became obvious that making a profit from such a venture would be a long haul – in the meantime, there were bills to pay for heating, lighting, insurance, etc. Harris had clearly bought a pig in a poke and it was in his interest to off load it as quickly as possible.

Enter UCD into the picutre. The college had spent years trying to consolidate on the 230 acre Belfield site and the authorities were, to put it mildly, surprised when they received a telephone call from Minister O'Rourke indicating that the government was willing to put up money for the purchase of Carysfort. Over the following weeks they felt under considerable pressure to agree to the proposal. At first they had no plans for the site and a number of possible options were explored. The most obvious was that Carysfort retain its education connection by moving the Higher Diploma in Education courses there, but that proposal faltered. The idea began to crystallise that it should be used by the Faculty of Commerce, preferably for a post-graduate business school. As it happened, this has turned out to be something of a masterstroke but not all the faculty members at the time were convinced of its merit. At one memorable faculty meeting, where opposition was voiced to move part of the faculty to Carysfort, it was forcefully pointed out to the staff that the Taoiseach himself favoured the idea.

The irony was not lost on the academics. The Government had had an opportunity to purchase Carysfort earlier and expressed no interest in it. Now, suddenly it was willing to put up £8m for the site. There was a double irony as UCD had, in the meantime, gone ahead with negotiations to purchase a site at Roebuck. There was no suggestion that the government would pay for the Roebuck purchase – UCD would have to find the funds itself to buy that site. But it was also clear that government money would be available for the purchase of Carysfort. This was an offer Dr Paddy Masterson, the College President, could hardly refuse. Mrs. O'Rourke argues forcefully that Carysfort was the better site from an educational point of view. If this was the case, however, why was this view not taken the previous June? Why was the final price paid so large, and most of all, why were the methods used so much at variance with normal practice?

Perhaps Mrs. O'Rourke or Charlie Haughey might help with an explanation to the Moriarity Tribunal.

Haughey had a heavy personal involvement in the discussions, which was not all that odd, since he had a track record for taking a detailed interest in other Ministers' work, but it was certainly odd in terms of the normal way of conducting government business.

Civil servants were excluded from the discussions between Haughey, O'Rourke and Masterson, which in itself was a breach of protocol. No fewer than eight private meetings took place between the three. But for Masterson's forthright testimony to the Dáil Committee on Public Accounts, much of what did become known might never have come to light. At an informal government meeting on December 4, Ministers agreed that their education and Finance colleagues should consider the use of the college as a school for business management, with possible support from the state. There was a major breach of normal procedures here, in that no memorandum was circulated to Ministers in advance so that their Departments could make their views known. Normally, all expenditure has to be approved by the Cabinet and in particular by the Minister for Finance.

Two weeks later, the Dept of Finance, under Albert Reynolds, agreed that a supplementary estimate for £9.7 million would be put before the Dáil for the purchase of Carysfort. There was little the Minister could do to question this expenditure, for the Dept of Education had already agreed to buy the property from Harris. Not only was the Dept of Finance unhappy about the price being paid; its jealously guarded constitutional right to be consulted on all state spending in advance had been over ridden.

Reynolds did stipulate that the new business college should be self-financing, with no subsidy for its running costs from either the State or UCD. But Masterson had already made clear to Haughey and O'Rourke that the proposed school would need continued support. The estimate included both the £8m purchase price and a further £1.7 million to help UCD prepare the building and set up the school.

Mrs. O'Rourke maintained that the informal government meeting showed there was no objection to the proposed purchase and cleared the way for her to negotiate it. There is no suggestion of any impropriety on her part. But, like many other Ministers who served under him, if Haughey wanted something and wanted it quickly, she dared not stand in his way.

By the usual government standards, things moved with remarkable speed. The supplementary estimate was put through the Dáil within days of Reynolds' approval. The money was passed on to the Higher Education Authority and special arrangements were put in place so that the cheque could be drawn and actually paid over to Harris's company on Christmas Eve. The Higher Education Authority handed over the money but it, too, was very annoyed because of lack of consultation in advance of the purchase, for such a major project should have come under its remit. Harris had now cleared a profit of £1.75 million in six months, thanks to the government decision that UCD must have the property for a school, even if it required state funds to buy and refurbish it. A site that had sold for £2 million had quadrupled in price in a very short time.

I wonder how Mr. Harris had this forthsight? Maybe, he could explain this to the Tribunal.

Haughey's supporters pointed to the fact that UCD had acquired excellent premises for a top class business school and labelled the people who criticised the deal as "the usual begrudgers." Opponents of the purchase - political and financial – believed the price was far too high.

16

TROUBLE WITH
THE FOURTH
ESTATE

Haughey's uneasy relations with the media go way back, almost to the start of his political career. One of the first controversies he became involved in concerned the sale of his home in Raheny for £204,000: – a figure worth ten times as much in today's money. It became an issue in the election of 1969 when the Labour candidate Conor Cruise O'Brien pointed out that the value of the house and 40 acres of land had rocketed from around £50,000 because he had been granted planning permission for house building though the land was situated in a green belt.

A photographer from one of the Dublin newspapers was sent to get a picture of the house. Mrs. Haughey answered the door but closed it without saying anything when he explained why he had come. The photographer decided to take pictures of the house anyway and was snapping away merrily when a Mercedes car swept into the driveway. Haughey got out and began to harangue him. Newspaper photographers are rough diamonds and this man is a veteran of many newsrooms. But he recalls: "I was subjected to a torrent of foul-mouthed abuse of a kind I've never heard before or since."

Haughey's ferocious tongue was one of his most notable characteristics. But it was rarely employed against members of the media. His own press officers were a different matter. Correspondents recall seeing Haughey abusing Frank Dunlop, then government press secretary, at an EU presidency meeting, over some perceived failure. Dunlop interrupted him: "If you keep going on like that, I'll walk away." Haughey continued his tirade, so Dunlop walked away with the Taoiseach shouting after him: "Don't you fucking walk away from me!" There is a less-known sequel to the story. The following day, Haughey rang Dunlop's wife, who was expecting a baby at the time, to inquire how she was getting on and to tell her everything was going well at the meeting. Whether this was meant an apology or not, no one knew.

Everyone agrees that Haughey's great gift was to keep people guessing so that they were never sure what he would do next. "He always seemed to have an innate sense of people's weaknesses," says one. "He always knew where to put the pressure. But if he was ultimately resisted, he would go at it a different way. He had endless ways of putting people under stress." In his youth, according to associates, he learnt lines of poetry, in Latin and Irish as well as English. He would quote these at appropriate moments, to civil servants and politicians, or journalists, knowing that very few would have enough education to respond in kind.

Haughey did not cultivate journalists in quite the same way as he did selected politicians, business and artistic people. A few hacks were permitted into the inner sanctum of Kinsealy for legendary late-night drinking sessions. But it was a precarious privilege, for they were always in dread of having their licence unceremoniously terminated at the whim of their host.

With journalists outside the charmed circle he had to be more circumspect. One of these was Bruce Arnold of the *Irish Independent*. Arnold had been trying to get an interview with Haughey for several days. He made his way into Government Buildings and as Haughey was walking down the corridor to his office, Arnold suddenly appeared from a side door and started asking questions. Haughey was perfectly polite. "I haven't got time now. Make an appointment." But when the journalist had been ushered away Haughey turned furiously on his officials. "Don't ever let him in here again!" he roared. Arnold never got the appointment.

Haughey was funny about interviews. There were things he did not want to discuss. The government press secretary from

1987, P J Mara, made an uncharacteristic slip during an official visit to Australia. Briefing journalists about what would happen and what questions they could ask, Mara quipped: "And no oul' Arms Trial shite!" Most of the Australian journalists had never heard of the 1970 trial when Haughey was charged and acquitted of illegally importing arms for use in Northern Ireland. But once alerted they were very very interested!

On the rare occasions when he did give interviews, journalists came to know some of Haughey's psychological tricks to gain the high ground. This usually consisted of saying at the last moment that he had decided not to do the interview, or even that he did not know who the journalist was. The idea may have been that, by the time the interview actually started, the desperate reporter would be glad to get anything from the man. Sometimes he would back down altogether. On one occasion he turned down the privilege of being interviewed for the leading French newspaper Le Monde. After much prevarication, he was finally unable to face being questioned by its tough Dublin correspondent, Joe Mulholland, now Director of Television RTE.

One story that has gone down in journalistic lore is that of an interview with a German crew working for the US network ABC. The crew was willing to submit written questions, which was perfect for Haughey, and of course the item would have a huge audience in the USA. But when they arrived for their morning appointment, Haughey refused to open his office door and responded to requests with: "Fuck off. Go away." Eventually an official discovered that the problem was not stage fright but a raging hangover from a night spent consuming copious quantities of vintage claret. Haughey was slumped over his desk holding the list of questions. "I can't do it," he muttered. "Tell them to go away." "Orange juice - black coffee," ordered the official and in due course Haughey recovered sufficiently to answer the questions. The Germans were very puzzled by the mysterious goings on but left reasonably happy with the result.

As the telephone tapping affair showed, Haughey was as obsessed with media coverage of himself and his administrations as any other politician. But his suspicions of journalists in general meant he was less active about briefing and leaking even to selected journalists, in the way that most politicians do. "I never knew him to leak anything," says one veteran correspondent. A major scoop in the *Evening Herald* during Lynch's premiership was put down to Haughey but in general he preferred to court cameramen and keep the reporters at bay. He was on good terms with many of the news photographers and, in turn, they often helped give him a good picture. He was vain about his appearance and preferred to be photographed from certain angles. He abhorred being pictured beside somebody taller than himself.

With reporters, relations were often more difficult. After one Ard Fheis (party conference) as was customary, Haughey came up to the press box. "You got a great reception tonight," said one reporter. Haughey looked at him suspiciously. "Do you begrudge me even that?" he flashed back. But he apologised later when he realised, to his surprise, that the praise had been genuine.

A Taoiseach's main contacts with the press are with the political correspondents who cover Leinster House. Haughey kept his distance from them but those who were in favour were invited to his office for background chats occasionally. Fianna Fáil's Christmas parties for the press were legendary for their liquid hospitality and for the season of goodwill, the political correspondents always got a present of a bottle of spirits – Tullamore Dew, Redbreast, Scotch House or even Bushmills – from Haughey personally. One, who may have been in disfavour at the time, went to Haughey's office to get his present. Haughey did not give it to him but gradually kept pushing it across the desk a little bit at a time as they were talking. Eventually, the confused hack had to move quickly to catch the bottle before it fell to the floor! He left in a sweat, clutching his hard won present.

17

THE SMEAR OF
THE FLAWED
PEDIGREE

The speech of former Progressive Democrat leader Des O'Malley in the Dáil in February 1999 was regarded as one of the finest. At last he could claim vindication for the stance he once took against Charles Haughey. Fifteen years before he had challenged the autocratic style of Haughey and was expelled from the National Executive of the Fianna Fáil for "conduct unbecoming."

In grave tones and with perfect timing he now delivered a very carefully written speech:

"Charles J. Haughey casts a long and dark shadow over Irish political life" he boomed. "It is nearly 20 years since he became Taoiseach and seven since he left public life, but our political system is still struggling to come to terms with his legacy."

He continued: "Charles Haughey took over the leadership of Fianna Fáil in 1979. He immediately set about stamping his particular style of leadership on that party and on the country. Both suffered as a result.

"Life in Fianna Fáil under Haughey was not exactly pleasant. If you disagreed with the leader's views you could be intimidated, threatened, even assaulted within the precincts of this House by his more thuggish supporters.

"Haughey sought to establish a close identification between the party and his own personality. At times even the nation, the party and himself became confused with each other in his mind. His leadership was based on a type of unquestioning personal loyalty demeaning to those who offered it, shallow to him who received it. Debate and discussion were discouraged, dissenting views were silenced. We were into the era of uno duce, una voce'.

"Charles Haughey created a new climate within Fianna Fáil, one very different to that which prevailed under his predecessors – Lynch, Lemass and de Valera. He created a climate of fear, a climate of greed, a climate of secrecy and conspiracy. The damage which Haughey was doing to the party and the country was becoming increasingly apparent as the years passed."

He then referred to his own problems with Haughey. "Many of us fought it. I was thrown out and others left, Deputy Molloy among them. Also among those who left was someone from the next political generation to ours, the Tanaiste, Deputy Harney. As a young person she had the courage and guts to stand up to Haughey, qualities which were sadly lacking in many of her more senior colleagues. Having said that, I am sure that if what is known now was known then there would have been many more who would have left with us.

"However, there were many who did not leave, many who felt totally comfortable in the kind of party which Charles Haughey had created. Among them was Mr. Padraig Flynn (the subject of a Dáil censure motion for not responding to allegations that he had received £50,000 from a County Sligo property developer).

"It might not be widely appreciated that Mr. Flynn and myself have something in common – we have both been dumped upon from a height by Fianna Fáil. It happened to me 15 years go. In 1984 I was expelled from the parliamentary party for my heretical views on Northern Ireland. The following year I was expelled from the party itself for my even more heretical views on the subject of family planning. On that occasion, Padraig Flynn was one of those doing the dumping. From the steps of party headquarters in Upper Mount Street, he addressed the nation through an RTE camera and pronounced that my conduct was 'unbecoming a member of Fianna Fáil'. Now it is Mr. Flynn's turn to be dumped upon."

Des O'Malley said that he could see more clearly why certain leading figures in Fianna Fáil, Mr. Flynn among them, were so opposed to the notion of coalition with the Progressive Democrats in 1989. "Could it be," he pondered, "that they were afraid that we would cramp their style of doing business?"

Turning to the future, Des O'Malley's gave his prognosis: "The next few months could be crucial in the political life of this country. We as a nation will be asked serious questions as to what kind of society we want, what kind of values we want and what kind of country we want. There may be further revelations made by tribunals, inquiries or the media of wrongdoing at the highest levels in Irish society. If there are, they may be shocking and disturbing to most members of the voting public.

"For example, to-day's newspapers report a Tribunal yesterday as having discovered that one of the providers of money – £100,000 – to a Haughey family company was Mr. Michael Murphy who had been a close associate of a long time insurance broker to Mr. Larry Goodman. He helped to negotiate Mr. Goodman's earliest export credit insurance cover for Iraq. He was also insurance broker to the Department of Agriculture and Food until it sued him last December in respect of huge losses it sustained in a major fire at a beef intervention store at Ballaghaderreen in 1992."

He spoke of the dilemma facing politicians: "They can choose to respond with courage, integrity and determination to eradicate the cancer of corruption that has poisoned the political and commercial affairs of this country in recent years – or they may choose to shirk their responsibility.

"They may choose to act the cute hoor' yet again. They may choose to turn a blind eye, look the other way and indicate their tacit toleration and acceptance of a culture of crookedness and corruption. The people of this country then have a choice.

"We may not have a general election for two or three years but events may dictate otherwise. Whenever the next election is held, the question of standards in public life is likely to be one of the main items on the political agenda, if not the main item."

He posed some questions for the electorate: "What kind of standards do people want? What kind of parties do they want? What kind of politicians do they want? Will they believe those who say that all these tribunals are only barrister-fattening exercises, a waste of time and money and that we do not want to be digging into all that class of thing in any event?"

He also had a question for his Fianna Fáil partners: " Would they vote for the brown envelope brigade if these gentlemen presented themselves for election again or are they prepared to make a genuine break with the past and embrace a new political order, one that gives precedence to decency over expediency, to honesty over dishonesty and to the public interest over the vested interest."

He concluded: "We have a chance to restore the public's faith in politics over the next few months and an opportunity to show that this Republic is run by decent people according to decent standards. Let us embrace that opportunity."

He was applauded by the small number of opposition deputies present and by one member of Fianna Fáil Dublin West TD, Liam Lawlor, who had temporarily drifted to O'Malley's side in one of the Haughey heaves.

The O'Malley speech in the Dáil had such an impact that the PD's doubled their support to four per cent at a subsequent opinion poll in the *Irish Times*.

It is opportune to recall another attack on Haughey, twenty years before. It was the famous "flawed pedigree" speech of Dr. Garrett FitzGerald, in December 1979, which he described at the time as one of the most difficult he had to make.

In contrast to his warm tribute on the retirement of former Taoiseach, Jack Lynch, whom he admired for his "tenacity and political skill" and his unique popularity as a political leader, Dr. FitzGerald did not mince his words when he spoke about his former university colleague, Charles Haughey.

Opposing a motion that Dáil Eireann nominate Deputy Charles J. Haughey for appointment by the President to be the Taoiseach, Dr. FitzGerald said: "The occasion of the election of a Taoiseach is not any ordinary debate. We are not here merely as representatives of parties seeking office in competition with one another on this occasion. My task is correspondingly difficult.

"In a way that has no precedent I am conscious of speaking for a large number of the Irish people, regardless of party, and I am very conscious of the difficulty of responding adequately and sensitively to this unique situation. I must speak not only for the Opposition but for many in Fianna Fáil who may not be free to say what they believe or to express their deep fears for the future of this country under the proposed leadership; people who are not free to reveal what they know and what led them to oppose this man. I hope that some at least may feel able to express their feelings, their very real patriotism and their deep concern for Ireland, but few or none may be able to do so. If that is the case, this task falls to others and, in the first instance, to me. I trust I may be equal to it, that I may say what needs to be said and can be said, recognising how much I cannot say, for reasons that all in this House understand."

In the public gallery listening to the FitzGerald speech was Mr. Haughey's elderly mother, his wife, Maureen and his four children.

He went on: "I take no pleasure in what I have to say. I have known Deputy Haughey for more than 35 years. I have never suffered insult or injury from him nor exchanged with him bitter words at any time. I would find my task today easier if we had not had this long relationship with each other, a relationship that was never intimate but never hostile. But I must do my duty regardless of these personal considerations. At the outset I must recognise his talents, his political skills and the competence he has shown in the past in the administration of Departments. These are important qualities in a Taoiseach, but they are not enough.

"This country has had six heads of Government since the State was founded. These were: William T. Cosgrave, Eamon de Valera, John A. Costello, Sean Lemass, Jack Lynch and Liam Cosgrave, all different kinds of men, God knows, but they all shared one common bond. They came into public life to serve this country and stayed on with that single purpose. None of them was ever alleged, even by his most unrelenting enemy (and some of them had unrelenting enemies on both sides) to have entered public life for any motive but the highest. Moreover, whatever their contemporary opponents may have said of them, whatever history's interim or later verdict on them may be, all were men who commanded the trust of those close to them. From a recollection of their virtues we may draw sustained hope for the future of this State."

Mr. Haughey's family in the public gallery winced as Dr. FitzGerald continued: "Deputy Haughey presents himself here, seeking to be invested in office as the seventh in this line, but he comes with a flawed pedigree. His motives can be judged ultimately only by God but he cannot ignore the fact that he differs from his predecessors in that these motives have been and are widely impugned, most notably but by no means exclusively, by people within his own party, people close to him who have observed his actions for many years and who have made their human, interim judgement on him. They and others, both in and out of public life, have attributed to him an overwhelming ambition, which they do not see as a simple emanation of a desire to serve, but rather as a wish to dominate, even to own, the State.

"This judgement will be contested by others. It cannot be more than an imperfect assessment of the man but it is incontestable that this view of him is widely and most passionately held by people in his own party. If elected, he will be the first in a line of hitherto patriotic men who will have been viewed in this way by many contemporaries and many of his colleagues."

Mr. Haughey sat impassively as the bitter words flowed from the Fine Gael leader. "The second aspect of the election of this man as Taoiseach which must disturb deeply every democrat is that, whatever may be the result of the vote and I think that is a foregone conclusion – he knows, I know and they all know that he does not command the genuine confidence of even one-third or this House never mind one half. No previous Taoiseach has been elected in similar circumstances.

"Formally, of course, he will secure a majority of votes. He will fulfil the constitutional requirement to form a government. He will then constitutionally be Taoiseach. As democrats we must respect the forms of democracy, even when the true spirit of the democratic system is not breathed into these forms. Though we must respect these forms we are entitled to comment on the emptiness of this formality.

"The feet that will go through that lobby to support his election will include many that will drag; the hearts of many who will climb those stairs before turning aside to vote will be heavy. Many of those who may vote for him will be doing so in the belief

111

and the hope that they will not have long to serve under a man they do not respect, whom they have fought long and hard, but for the moment in vain, to exclude from the highest office in the land. These men and women who, while they may give their formal consent, withhold their full consent in the interior forum, include a clear majority of those who have served with him in government, who know his abilities better than most but are repelled by other defects which they see as superseding all considerations of mere competence, political skill or adroitness.

"Who are the men – three out of ten Members of this assembly – who have placed their full confidence in Deputy Haughey, electing him to the leadership of his party? Oddly they include the members of the party opposite who, whatever criticism may be and has been made by us and others of their political judgement, are recognised outside their party and within it as people of integrity. Do they include the Taoiseach, because he is still Taoiseach until his successor is elected? Do they include Deputy Colley, Deputy O'Malley, Deputy O'Donoghue, Deputy Wilson, Deputy Faulkner, Deputy Dennis Gallagher, Deputy Molloy, Deputy Woods? I need not continue with the list and no one need feel slighted if I omit honorable names. These are people who are respected outside Fianna Fáil and within for their genuine patriotism however much we on these benches may at times have to question their judgement or the wisdom of their policies in the national interest.

"It is not from such as these that Deputy Haughey won his majority. His majority comprises men judged inadequate in office in the past; men ambitious for office but disappointed hitherto; men fearful of losing office because they backed the wrong horse; and, above all, at least 18 men who scraped home narrowly in 1977 and who, fearing for the seats that were so unexpectedly won for them by the gamble of the manifesto, have now switched their bet to another gamble, the gamble of Deputy Haughey."

He was then interrupted by the Ceann Comhairle who told him that the motion before the House concerned the suitability of Deputy Charles Haughey, Minister for Health and Social Welfare, for the office of Taoiseach. "Members who may or may not have supported him are not under discussion."

But Dr. FitzGerald was not detracted. "We are electing the leader of this State and I will not be silenced in doing my duty in this House as I see it. I want to say one thing more in fairness to Deputy Haughey's supporters. Not all of them are drawn from these categories. They include also a few people who are not personally motivated, but who are inspired by a narrow and dangerous nationalism that is the antithesis of everything Tone and Davis stood for, a patriotism that effectively – even if they do not admit it to themselves, excludes one million Irish men and women from the nation as they conceive it; men and women who do not believe in seeking unity by agreement but who crave after unity by constraint; men and women who – whether they themselves realise it or not – think in terms of imposing one Irish tradition on those who, with their ancestors for generations past, had honoured a different but also an Irish tradition. These men and women who voted for Deputy Haughey on grounds of idealism misplaced as I see it and free from personal interest are, I believe and the great majority of almost five million Irish people believe, not merely misguided but dangerously misguided.

"Taken together these groups of self interested and fatally misguided defectors from the Republican tradition of 1798 and 1848 make up three Deputies out of every ten in this House. Yet, this motley minority may, and I think will, at the end of this debate make this man Taoiseach.

"Why so? The Irish people are entitled to ask this question. What worries me is whether I can honestly answer, if asked what the reason is, other than that, though many on both sides of His House have honourably struggled to break free from Civil War politics, nevertheless these politics, through the shackles of the party system that emerged from that Civil War, still bind some of the Members of this House in thralldom.

"If those on both sides of this House who see the dangers for this State that are almost inexorably and fatally embedded in the nomination now before us cannot find it possible at this moment to come together in face of this danger and make common cause for Ireland, can we truthfully say to our electorate, some of them born almost 40 years after that event, that there is any reason for this other than the origins of the parties to which we belong, –

origins that many of us had hoped were now totally irrelevant to the contemporary political life of this State?

"The long shadow of that darkest hour of our history, when Irishman fought Irishman, when families were divided, brother against brother, husband in conflict with wife – as happened in my own family – that long shadow which many of us had led ourselves to believe had long since lifted, darkens our understanding here to-day and inhibits this House from dividing along the lines of deepest conviction, along the lines that divide those who honestly seek Irish unity by agreement, and by agreement only, from those who, while they talk of peaceful means, still think at least subconsciously of constraint. It also divides true patriots from mere political opportunists.

"I would like to believe that there is still hope, still a possibility, that we could face this crisis in our affairs, throwing off these shackles and coming out from under this shadow. Perhaps it is too much to hope of men and women who are under intolerable pressures of tradition and convention at this point. However, if it does not happen today, that does not mean that it may not happen at some point in the middle future. For the mixture of men and motives artificially concocted to create a formal majority for Deputy Haughey when this debate ends must be frail and fragile; it cannot survive indefinitely the pressures on it imposed by his – I must say it – flawed character.

"There will be those around Deputy Haughey who will scoff, or perhaps purport to scoff, at these reflections. Some of them who see power as an end in itself rather than as a means to serve the public interest, may claim to see in what I have just said nothing more than regret that we on this side of the House cannot come to power now through a realignment of forces. They are welcome to this interpretation which would accord with their view of politics.

"But others will understand that I have spoken in these terms not from ambition but from conviction. Yes, I and those around me have the ambition to serve this country in office, a task for which we are seeking to prepare ourselves. But we can bide our time, all the more confident in the verdict of the people because of the choice inflicted on Fianna Fáil by a narrow majority of its members in circumstances which are already the subject of bitter recrimination within that party. I know that those who chose Deputy Haughey for the most part did so because they thought it to their electoral advantage. They will, I believe live to rue that misjudgement. By their action they have torn asunder their party, and no amount of patching or crack papering can put it together again whole, so long as Deputy Haughey remains its Leader. These divisions will have inevitable electoral consequences, consequences that they have failed to foresee, so confident were they that, if only their candidate could be bulldozed into the leadership, all would be well.

"If I were speaking here in party terms, if I were thinking narrowly in terms of the welfare of this party, I should be welcoming in a relaxed way the imminent advent to power of Deputy Haughey. I know that many decent people in every part of Ireland who have cast their votes for Fianna Fáil candidates are repelled by the thought of Deputy Haughey in power and, however skillfully and energetically he may strive, during the next year or two years, to apply his undoubted talents to the task of Government, he will not persuade these people to cast their votes for a party led by him, even if that party were to be a united one, which palpably it will not be.

"But if Deputy Haughey as Taoiseach is an uncovenanted bonus to Fine Gael, a precipitating factor that will bring to our support many good and patriotic people of integrity who for many years have cast their votes for Fianna Fáil under Deputy Jack Lynch, he cannot be seen in the same light so far as the national interest is concerned. On this occasion I have to say, with regret even some bitterness that the interests of my party and the nation do not coincide. I have the interest of this nation sufficiently at heart I think in saying that I speak for my party also to prefer to take our chance with another Fianna Fáil leader who would not provoke such mistrust amongst the electorate and who would be correspondingly harder to beat, than for the country to have to take a chance with Deputy Haughey.

"Why is it such a chance? There are many reasons. I shall give only a few; some are not to be raised even in this privileged assembly. The first is that there is a question-mark that remains over a man who was accused of conspiracy to import arms to the IRA and after he had been found not guilty of that charge chose

115

to seek the plaudits of the crowd for a man who represented that organisation at that time, saying of him: "he is one of the finest persons I have known in all my time in public life and politics". For nine long years after that day – nine long years – he refused to utter one word of condemnation of the IRA until faced with a question on this issue at a press conference following his election to the leadership of his party. I say "refused" advisedly. Deputy Haughey disingenuously told his questioner at the press conference on Friday that the reason he had never expressed any condemnation of the IRA up to that moment was that responsibility in regard to Northern Ireland policy has been something for the Taoiseach and the Minister for Foreign Affairs".

"In what way, I ask the House, would that allocation of responsibility preclude any Minister in an Irish Government from expressing his abhorrence of the IRA for its murders and robberies North and South, its orgy of destruction, its threat to our democratic institutions, institutions which it refuses to recognise in this State and which its spokesmen recently threatened to destroy? If Deputy Haughey abhorred the IRA and wished, as any decent man would wish to do, to clear his name of any sympathy with them after the experience or being accused of conspiring to import arms for their benefit, he could have done so at any moment since that trial ended, in full accord with the policy of successive Governments. He chose, most deliberately, not to do so. He refused to entertain questions on this issue from journalists. He preferred to maintain an indecent ambiguity over his attitude until safely ensconced in the leadership of his party. Did he fear that if he had any earlier than Friday afternoon last said the words "I condemn the Provisional IRA and all their activities" he might have received less enthusiastic support for his candidature from some of the – the politest word is greener – members of his party? Now that he has the job, does he feel he can safely condemn what he was so careful to avoid condemning for nine long years? The question mark on this issue which Deputy Haughey has chosen deliberately to allow to linger around him for all those years is one reason – the highest of all reasons – for refusing him confidence. It is one reason why so many of his colleagues do not have confidence in him.

The second reason is that, arising from this deliberate ambiguity Deputy Haughey, as leader of his party and, perhaps, soon as Taoiseach, is and will be an obstacle to Irish unity to be achieved by agreement. No one with that background of silence – to put it no higher – could by any stretch of the imagination, offer reassurance to Northern Protestants looking southwards, as many have begun to do, in search of a permanent solution in conjunction with the people of this part of Ireland. As an Irish nationalist who, I believe, with the exception of Deputy Harte, has devoted more time than any other Member of this House to the cause of peace in Ireland and to a new political relationship between North and South, I cannot endorse the candidature of a man who seeks to be Taoiseach of this State, but who in that capacity will represent a barrier to unity by agreement.

"Thirdly, while I have already remarked on Deputy Haughey's political ability and administrative competence, he has shown himself – especially and most relevantly in this decade – more concerned with public relations and less with achievement than is acceptable in a Minister. He has been in the Departments of Health and Social Welfare. He neglected the latter Department almost totally, while in the former he dragged his feet on all awkward issues, from contraceptive regulations to nurses' pay, putting in time until his moment should come to replace the man he had for so long worked to undermine. In passing, I must repeat what I said on the Bill dealing with contraception – that this legislation by the very terminology it contains and uses to describe forms of family planning, is denominational. By its introduction Deputy Haughey reinstitutionalised denominationalism in Irish legislation in total disregard of the principles of republicanism, at least as Tone and Davis understood them and in equal disregard of the interest of bringing North and South together which he claims to be committed to. On the blatant hypocrisy of this Bill, taken in conjunction with his protestations of republicanism that suddenly blossomed for the Padraig Pearse centenary, he deserves to be rejected as Taoiseach of this State, a State whose people aspire to unity by agreement between the people of North and South.

"The fourth and final reason why Deputy Haughey is to be

rejected, is his failure to articulate any idealism that might inspire the younger generation and because of his own life style. This failure to articulate any idealism that might inspire that generation makes him particularly unfitted for the task of leading into the eighties a State half of whose population are under 25 years of age.

"It is on those four grounds, amongst others to which I do not propose to refer, that I propose the rejection of Deputy Haughey's nomination as Taoiseach.

"I have not found that speech easy to make. It is distasteful to have to argue the merits of an individual rather than a policy and to reflect so critically on the performance and character of a parliamentary colleague I have known for many years. I am conscious also of the tension between the duty I owe to the State in speaking frankly on these matters and the duty I owe to Parliament not to overstep the mark by entering into areas inappropriate for debate, or by using harsher language than is minimally called for by the occasion. I am sure that fault may be found on both grounds with what I have said and I beg the indulgence of the House if I have offended in either respect. I have had to decide where my duty lay and although I have seen public advice offered as to the desirability or not of making such comments, I have had to decide in the interest of the State as I see it to reject that advice and to take any criticism that may come as a result.

" I move, in the name of my party, and on behalf also, I believe, of many who will have to remain silent during this debate, and may not even feel free to vote with their feet according to their inclinations, the rejection of the nomination of Deputy Haughey."

During the debate on the Presidential election in 1990, the then Labour leader, Dick Spring launched a fierce attack on Haughey in Dáil Eireann.

Spring made the speech on the 31st of October 1990 after the election of President Mary Robinson. The campaign had been thrown into turmoil by the sensational publication of a taped interview with the Fianna Fáil candidate, the late Brian Lenihan. A U.C.D. student had interviewed Lenihan about telephone calls to Aras an Uachtarain in 1982. The tape, which was in the possession of *The Irish Times*, was played to journalists at a press conference in Dublin.

During the presidential campaign, Lenihan had denied that he or other leading members of Fianna Fáil had tried to contact President Hillery by phone at Aras an Uachtarain on the night of 27th of January, 1982, when Garret FitzGerald's first budget had collapsed, in an attempt to persuade him not to dissolve the Dáil. But, in the taped interview Lenihan let slip that he had a phone conversation with the President on the night in question and that Charles Haughey had tried to ring the President the same night.

The army officer on duty at the Aras, Captain Ollie Barbour had taken all the phone calls and refused to put anyone through on President Hillery's instructions. One of the phone calls had been from Haughey himself and included a peremptory instruction to "put me through to the President". When Captain Barbour refused, Haughey told him that he would be Taoiseach again one day and "when I am I intend to roast your fucking arse if you don't put me through immediately". Dr. Hillery was so concerned at this threat that he subsequently exercised his prerogative as Commander-in-Chief of the armed forces to instruct the Chief of Staff of the Defence Forces to place a note on the army officer's personnel file, to the effect that none of the events of the night in question were ever to be seen as reflecting any discredit on the officer's record and that everything he had done had been on the express instructions of the President.

In the subsequent Dáil debate on the tapes, Charles Haughey told the Dáil, his voice breaking with emotion, that he himself had never abused an army officer. His father, he said, had served in the Defence Forces and anyone who could possibly believe that he would abuse an army officer knew nothing of the deep respect he held for the army.

The release of the tape caused a political sensation with less than a week to go to polling day. Lenihan compounded his problems by giving radio and television interviews in which he maintained that what he said on the tape was not the truth and that he had never rung the Aras. He later explained in his book

"For the Record" (written by columnist Angela Phelan) that he had been on heavy medication at the time of the interview, following his liver transplant operation a year earlier and that accounted for his story. But he didn't provide that explanation at the critical juncture of the campaign and things began to come apart.

His partners in Government – the Progressive Democrats – told Charles Haughey that the price of their support was Brian Lenihan's resignation. Lenihan refused to resign and was sacked by his long time friend, Haughey.

It was Dick Spring's view that Haughey should resign himself, rather than throw his closest political friend and supporter to the wolves to save his skin. There was no Government member present when Spring stood up in the Dáil to make his speech. He told the gathering: "Over the weekend a commentator wrote that I was wrong in my assessment made last week that it was a sad week for Irish politics. I still feel I was right and that last week was a sad week for Irish politics. What is going on at the moment is sad for politics and politicians. Let us hope that after this there will be some light ahead for politics and the standards in political life. I am not convinced of that as things stand.

"I have to say at the outset that I am astonished that the Taoiseach has chosen to treat the matter which has given rise to this debate with such contempt. He has contented himself with repeating the brazen denials of the past week in circumstances where the entire country has made it clear that they do not believe those denials. He has tried to ensure that the central issue is the personality of Brian Lenihan. It is not – Brian Lenihan is liked and admired on all sides of this House on a personal basis, but he cannot be regarded as being immune from the need for high political standards simply because he is a nice man.

"The Taoiseach has compounded the arrogance of his bare-faced denials by indulging himself in a whole series of unworthy smears against people who are Members of this House, and two who are not. His remarks about Mary Robinson are typical of some of the dirt that is being flung by Fianna Fáil speakers around the country in their panic at the imminent prospect of being beaten in a fair contest."

Then came bitter rhetoric: "This debate is not about Brian Lenihan, when it is all boiled down. This debate, essentially is about the evil spirit that controls one political party in this Republic, and it is about the way in which that spirit has begun to corrupt the entire political system in our country. This is a debate about greed for office, about disregard for truth and about contempt for political standards. It is a debate about the way in which a once great party has been brought to its knees by the grasping acquisitiveness of its leader. It is ultimately a debate about the cancer that is eating away at our body politic and the virus which has caused that cancer, An Taoiseach, Charles J. Haughey."

He went on: "In the 1989 General Election, I said that Fianna Fáil was a party that had become stultified in the grip of one man. As I have watched the events of the last week unfold, in common with thousands of other mystified and outraged citizens of the country, the conviction has been borne in on me more and more that Fianna Fáil is incapable of recovering its former stature for as long as that man is in a position to exert a stranglehold on the party. I have watched the elected Taoiseach of our country tell lies to the Dáil, and brazenly accuse others of lying when he knew the accusations were false; I have watched the Tanaiste try to turn himself into an Irish version of Richard Nixon, staring straight into television cameras and telling lies to the entire nation without so much as a blink".

The Ceann Comhairle interrupted him: "I am concerned about the reference to lies. The standing convention in this House is that deliberate falsehoods should not be attributed to any Member."

Mr. Spring: "I am sure the nation shares your concern about lies but at this stage convention in this House has been turned on its ear, unfortunately".

An Ceann Comhairle: "The Chair will still strive to uphold the traditions of this House."

Mr. Spring:"I appreciate your dilemma, a Cheann Comhairle."

Dick Spring continued: "I have watched a succession of Ministers and official Government spokesmen participate in a total and sustained effort to deceive the people who elected them, and as I have watched, I have wondered, as I am sure many thousands of others have wondered, what kind of country have we become. Could it be that these people have simply lost sight of the difference between truth and lies? Or could it be that they have chosen to lie their way, deliberately and casually, out of political embarrassment simply because they have come to believe they can get away with anything? If that is the case, how has it happened that these elected representatives have developed so much contempt for their electorate that they feel free to tell so many lies?

"Let us be quite clear: we have been lied to so often that there is virtually nothing that we can believe in any more. The Taoiseach and his Ministers are like characters from Alice in Wonderland telling us that the truth is whatever they say it is – no more, no less; but we do not live in Wonderland – we live in a democracy where trust in the political system depends ultimately on the truth told by politicians. If truth cannot be relied upon, then democracy ultimately will crumble.

"The issues that have been raised in the last week are not new. Many of them arise from stories that have been going the rounds for years. But it is a measure of the cynicism of Fianna Fáil that having ignored the stories for years, they should choose to deny them flatly at any moment when they might cause embarrassment. And when confronted with incontrovertible proof that lies had been told, they simply, and with total arrogance, asserted that anyone pointing to the proof was maliciously motivated.

"This is a simple technique. It was (used) by Josef Goebbels in Nazi Germany, and subsequently elaborated by Senator Joe McCarthy in the United States. Both of these politicians had a number of things in common – they both believed that democracy was capable of being twisted to their own ends and they both believed in the efficacy of the big lie.

"In the end, both of these politicians destroyed themselves, but not before they had perverted the society in which they lived. And that is the danger we face here – for the last week, and more, we have been in a virtual tailspin of lies and mismanagement, with the situation becoming daily more out of control. The corrupting effect of the political cynicism that we have been watching cannot be overstated. If it is allowed to continue, it will cause long term and lasting damage to our concept of, and commitment to, parliamentary democracy in Ireland.

"In the last week, in addition to all the lies, we have all heard one Fianna Fáil Junior Minister, Michael Smith, deliver a rabble-rousing speech to a Fianna Fáil meeting in Edenderry that was as close as anything I have heard to a fascist tub-thumper from the thirties. At a different meeting in Wexford, those who were there (and they included Fianna Fáil presidential candidate Brian Lenihan) were no doubt privileged to hear another Fianna Fáil Deputy, John Browne, exhort his members to ensure that Mary Robinson was never in a position 'to open an abortion referral clinic in Aras An Uachtarain'. Increasingly, reports are coming in from journalists that Fianna Fáil meetings these days are frightening occasions for the neutral participants.

"Members of a political party who can behave like this have clearly lost any sense they ever had of what is true or decent or honorable. It must not be allowed to develop, for the sake of all of us. We had plenty of it in the twenties and thirties but it must stop. It must be stopped by the authority of this House and by the leader of that party, for everybody's sake, before we are into an unstoppable mess.Some Fianna Fáil people will undoubtedly see this as little more than the Party fighting back, in the middle of a Presidential campaign that they are clearly losing. But many more Fianna Fáil, in their hearts, know that this is a debased and degrading form of politics. When politics depends on lies and smears to survive, it is little more than the politics of the gutter.

"There has been much talk about the need to restore the credibility of the Government – but surely the fact is that the credibility of politics is more important than the fate of any one Government.

"There is an ethos underlying Fianna Fáil politics now. It is that ethos that forced Des O'Malley and others out of Fianna Fáil. It is not the ethos of Sean Lemass, Jack Lynch or George Colley. It is, instead, the ethos so clearly illustrated on the Brian Lenihan Late Late Show, when the audience was invited to chuckle at stories of how Brian dealt with "a sharp little bitch" who happened to be a nun, or of how gardaí were threatened with disciplinary action for trying to carry out their jobs.

"No doubt the same ethos informed the Taoiseach when, as it

has been alleged, he rang Aras an Uachtarain in January 1982 and threatened to end the career of a member of the Army if the officer concerned did not put him through to the President. If it was proved that a member of Provisional Sinn Fein made that telephone call he could be sentenced to seven years penal servitude but when the Leader of Fianna Fáil does it we are supposed to accept it as part of the way we run our politics. Having heard his denial in his speech just now can we assume – and I will be insisting – that he will now institute a Garda inquiry into the matter in order to clear his name? Such a step would carry far more weight than the high-flown rhetoric we have just heard from him.

"I said a moment ago that we are supposed to regard all this as the way politics is run in Ireland. I do not and I hope I never do. I believe there are many in Fianna Fáil also who do not. That party can claim credit for many great achievements in the economic and social development of Irish life. It is a party which has been radical in its day and never slow to adopt new ideas. But, in the last 11 years, it has become a party dedicated to the oldest idea in politics – the idea of power for its own sake, vested in the imperial and dictatorial ambitions of its leader. Thus, dissent and even debate has been silenced; all hint of criticism is seen as betrayal; any political campaign waged against the party is seen as anti-Irish. It is one of the most striking features of the modern-day Fianna Fáil that not one of their elected representatives has had the courage to say in the middle of the present mess that enough is enough. Even though privately, many accept that the last week or so has been a tissue of lies and deceit, not one of them is prepared to offer the slightest public criticism. Instead they troop in here this morning like sheep, and applaud the most outrageous and unsustainable utterances of their leader. In the modern Fianna Fáil, even loyalty has become debased to the most shameless sycophancy.

"This last week would not have happened in the days of Sean Lemass or of Jack Lynch. It would not have happened if there had been a George Colley or any person of stature and honour left on the Fianna Fáil benches. How can anyone conceive of all this happening in the days of the founder of Fianna Fáil, and the author of our Constitution, Eamon de Valera? But they have all gone, and the party is now dedicated to the greed and unprincipled behaviour of its present leader, who is bent on creating a party entirely in his own image. When the world watched Ceaucescu and Honecker fall, we knew it was because people could no longer tolerate tyranny but how much longer will the members of Fianna Fáil tolerate the internal tyranny that rules their party with an iron hand and that has brought it to a point where it is an object of shame and revulsion for so many?

"Speaking in this House on the day this Government was formed, on 12 July 1989, I said the following:

'Over the next months and years, two main questions will preoccupy the political system of our country. At least, these two questions ought to be among the principal issues that we face and deal with. It may well be that these issues will be ignored, and that they will be settled by default. It may well be that the politicians we have elected to Government will simply turn a blind eye to them, and allow them to be decided by faceless, anonymous people. If that were to happen, the result would be disastrous, as it has been disastrous in other countries where these issues have arisen.

The questions are these: first, how are the fruits of economic growth to be distributed and, secondly who is going to wield the power and influence of ownership in Ireland in the future?

These are huge and difficult questions. They may not seem at first glance to be the most obvious ones that arise on a day like this but if recent political experience has shown us anything, it has shown us that issues like these must be pushed to the centre of the political stage. Too much of our recent experience has been tied up with defending people against the callous and unthinking consequences of an ill-considered approach to policy. Too much of our recent experience has been tied up with unscrambling the consequences of secret deals and political cronyism. We cannot, as a community, allow the style and substance of this kind of Government to continue.'

"Little did I know what would arise after that Government were formed and why we are all here today. I believed then that despite the presence in Government of a party who have the protection of high political standards on their agenda, there was every possibility that the style of Government we have come to

125

associate with Mr. Haughey would predominate. And what has happened? Mr. Haughey has stood by while the Cathaoirleach of the Seanad –"

An Ceann Comhairle: "I am sorry to interrupt the Deputy but Standing Orders of this House ordain that Members shall be referred to by their appropriate titles, of Taoiseach, Tanaiste, Deputy, Minister or Junior Minister as the case may be."

Mr. Spring: "A Cheann Comhairle, I take your correction. The Taoiseach, Mr. Charles J. Haughey, stood by while the Cathaoirleach of the Seanad, Senator Sean Doherty, completely misled that House, concealing vital information from it in a manner that threatened to pervert the course of natural justice and bring that House into disrepute."

An Ceann Comhairle: "Matters appertaining to the other House should not be referred to here, Deputy Spring. It is not usual to do so."

Mr. Spring: "With all due respects, a Cheann Comhairle, Mr. Haughey has gone well outside this House this morning in referring to many other things."

An Ceann Comhairle: " The Taoiseach."

Mr. Spring: "... The Taoiseach has, and I intend to follow that course as well. The Taoiseach was silent while another Member of the Seanad, Senator Dr. Sean Mc Carthy abused his constitutional protection to avoid a drunk driving charge."

An Ceann Comhairle:"Please, Deputy Spring, it is not appropriate that matters appertaining to the Seanad should be referred to in such a derogatory fashion here."

Mr. Spring: "Certainly I believe they are worthy of comment in this debate on such a fundamental issue."

An Ceann Comhairle: "They should be left to the other House."

Mr. Spring: "If I had confidence in the other House I would do so but I do not. The Taoiseach has ignored all the well-founded allegations of political favouritism that have surrounded the Goodman affair, choosing to attack foreign banks rather than face the reality that his closeness with Mr. Goodman gave one entrepreneur the opportunity to construct an empire built on sand.

"The Taoiseach has had absolutely nothing to say while Patrick Gallagher (a builder and a close friend of Haughey's) has walked away from prosecution in the Republic. I have here in my possession the report of the liquidator in the case of Merchant Banking Limited. It lists no fewer than 22 areas in which offences may have been committed, including bribery and conspiracy. Questions will always surround this case in which so many people lost their life savings. Yet, the Taoiseach has refused to institute an inquiry into those legitimate questions.

"These are some instances only of the way in which this Government have discharged the mandate they received from the people. It is a dishonourable record which we have consistently opposed. It has been said in defence of the Government – and the Taoiseach has repeated here this morning– that they have been successful in economic terms. In that regard, I would have to say nothing has been achieved by this Government, no economic miracle has been wrought without a very considerable price having been paid by many people in our community. In the main, that price has been paid by those least able to bear it. In health, education and other essential services like housing it is the old, the sick and the handicapped who have borne the cost of the so-called economic recovery. In the main, it has been multi-national companies and the financial services sector that have benefited from the economic growth. But, just as the Taoiseach was unaware during the election campaign of 1989 that the health services were in a state of crisis, just as he admitted on radio that he did not realise so many people were in difficulty by way of lack of access to our health services, I can assure him the same awaits him on doorsteps now. There have been no improvements whatever brought about in our health services since the election of this Government.

"Public housing is facing a crisis. Urgent steps must be taken in that regard but nothing has been done. I do not believe the Taoiseach appreciates the serious mess that awaits him if he goes out on the road from this House today.

"The Taoiseach referred in his speech to the new consensus between the social partners that has helped considerably in addressing economic problems but this Government seems intent on destroying that consensus with their programme of privatisation by stealth and with their insidious attacks on public enterprise.

"I have no confidence in this Taoiseach or Government. I cannot believe what he or the Government say and I believe there is a majority in this House who would agree with me. Indeed, I believe there is a majority in this country who would agree with that statement. It may be a secret and silent majority or it may not; we shall have to wait and see. In any event, I believe the people of Ireland as a whole have been hurt by the damage done to this country by the events of the past ten days to a point where the people can no longer have confidence in this Government. This Government must go."

—-oOo—-

In contrast to Des O'Malley, Dr. Garret FitzGerald and the Labour leader, Dick Spring, Dublin Central TD Tony Gregory had a different view of Charles Haughey.

He had intimate dealings with the former Taoiseach in February 1982 when they finalised the controversial "Gregory deal" – a package of commitments to Dublin Central constituency, worth a couple of hundred million pounds.

Gregory, an Independent who was to hold the balance of power for almost ten months, had six meetings at his constituency office – 20 Summerhill Parade – with Mr. Haughey. He also had a couple of meetings with the then Taoiseach, Dr. Garret FitzGerald, who was anxious for his support to keep the outgoing Coalition Government in power.

Said Tony Gregory: "Haughey was somebody you could warm to easily. He had the human touch. He was a very clever individual when he wanted to charm people. But if he did not like people, he knew how to walk on them."

Haughey was driven to the negotiations in Summerhill by his then Chief Whip, Bertie Ahern, later to become Taoiseach. He left Ahern in the car and handled the negotiations himself. Tony Gregory wanted transparency in the negotiations, so he brought along four of his colleagues to the talks.

There was in sharp contrast to the negotiations between Dr. FitzGerald and Mr. Haughey. Tony Gregory gave a list of demands to both politicians. According to Gregory, Dr. FitzGerald did not respond "in any realistic way to what we were saying". Haughey

128

spoke to officials in Dublin Corporation, including his brother, Sean, who was an assistant manager, sounding out what could be delivered to the constituency in terms of housing and jobs.

Added Tony Gregory: "When Haughey came back to us, we knew he had done his homework. He was trying to plamase us into supporting him. A few of us did not trust Haughey, because we knew of his reputation. We asked Mickey Mullins, then General Secretary of the I.T.G.W.U., to witness the deal being signed."

The deal was signed the night before the Dáil ratified Haughey as Taoiseach. After the deal was completed, Haughey turned around to Tony Gregory, Mickey Mullins and Gregory's four colleagues and said: "As Al Capone once said it was nice doing business with you!"

The Haughey Government collapsed in November 1982 after the Workers Party representatives withdrew their support. In the confidence vote, Tony Gregory abstained. In the debate on the confidence motion, Tony Gregory told the Dáil: "I want to put on record that regardless of what is being said about Haughey, in his dealings with me he behaved with honour and kept to his commitments."

After Tony Gregory had spoken, Charles Haughey walked up the steps of the Dáil gallery to personally thank him for what he had said.

Tony Gregory replied: "I would not have said it, if it was not the truth."

18

FIANNA FÁIL IN AMERICA

When Mr. Haughey's successor, Albert Reynolds became Taoiseach in February 1992, his top priority was to bring peace to Northern Ireland and steer the country's economic ship to even calmer waters. He had another urgent task that had little to do with the general public. The party finances were in a deplorable state, with a crippling debt close to £4m. One of his first tasks was to disband most of the Haughey fund raising committee. Out went Paul Kavanagh together with Mr. Haughey's daughter Eimear and the former Director General of Bord Failte Joe Malone.

The new Taoiseach took on board a suggestion of mine – a memorandum on how the enormous goodwill that exists in America could be turned to Ireland's benefit. Almost fifty per cent of the Chief Executives of Corporate America are of Irish extraction – an enormous resource never fully tapped or explored by an Irish Government. I suggested that the Irish Semi State bodies could research these high profile executives and find out who might be encouraged to invest in Ireland. Once the research was complete, they should be contacted individually by the Taoiseach, touching sensitive egos. They would be particularly chuffed at being personally contacted by the Irish Prime Minister.

Reynolds took the suggestion on board, developing it even further. He established a high profile Economic Committee whose job was to prepare a marketing policy for Ireland and act as a sounding board for ideas and policies. In the event of industrial problems, the Taoiseach could use the network of contacts to defuse any serious situation. This Economic Committee included Ireland's richest and most successful businessman, Dr. Tony O'Reilly, Chairman and Chief Executive of HJ Heinz and Independent Newspapers, Ltd., Roy Disney boss of the Walt Disney Company, former Coca Cola Chief Donald Keough, Fruit of the Loom boss John Holland, billionaire Chuck Feeney of Medallion Hotels, Bill Flynn of Mutual of America, Michael J. Roarty of Anheuser-Busch, Dan Rooney, owner of the Pittsburgh Steelers; General Electric boss John Welch, Peter Lynch of Fidelity Investments, Daniel Tully of Merrill Lynch & Co., Margaret Duffy of Arthur Anderson, Kerry-born Denis Kelleher of Wall Street Investor Services, Peter Lynch of Fidelity Investments, Mary Maguire of the Chase Manhattan Bank, Brian Thompson of LUI International, John Mc Gillicuddy of Chemical Banking Corporation, Daniel E. Gill of Bausch & Lomb in Rochester, Brian Burns of BF Enterprises, San Francisco, Boston businessmen Edmund Keely of Liberty Mutual Group, William Connell, boss of the Connell Limited Partnership and Donald Brennan, boss of Morgan Stanley Banking Group, Andrew McKenna of Schwarz Paper Company, Illinois, and John Patrick Casey of KPMG Peat Marwick, New York. Some years previously at a brief meeting, I made similar suggestions to Mr. Haughey, though not in writing, but Mr. Haughey took no action on the initiative.

In fairness, Mr. Haughey was the first Irish Taoiseach to establish a party fund-raising committee in the States. In charge of the operation was his first cousin, Barbara O'Neill, wife of the Cork-born New York restaurateur and publican, Terry O'Neill. The former Director General of Bord Failte, Mayo-born Joe Malone, was added. And Mr. Haughey sent Naoimh O'Connor, a daughter of his old friend and solicitor Pat O'Connor, to explore new ways of getting money to support Fianna Fáil activities. Initially, the group did well. The first $500-a-plate fund raising event in the exclusive Racing Club in New York was a huge success. Charles Haughey was piped into the room and the evening was described as one of the most sophisticated ever held by Fianna Fáil. One of the guests picked up the bill. Some who attended were promised lucrative Government contracts in return for their support.

As the American committee was launched, the Taoiseach was deeply sceptical of the advice being given by the establishment within the Department of Foreign Affairs on the Northern Ireland issue. Haughey wanted the Irish Ambassador to Washington, Sean Donlon, moved. He believed that Donlon exceeded his brief in criticising the Irish National Caucus, headed by Sean McManus and Noraid. The success of Donlon in influencing both the Carter administration and Congress had infuriated the Irish republican lobby, who had been effectively marginalised by his efforts. These republican groups looked to the new leader of Fianna Fáil and head of the Irish Government, Charles Haughey, to vindicate their cause by getting rid of the ambassador who had so effectively opposed them. At the end of June in 1980, Sean Donlon was called back to Dublin and told that he was being moved to the post of Permanent Representative to the United Nations in New York. However a major complication arose when the proposed moved was opposed by the hugely influential "Four Horsemen" – Tipp O'Neill, Ted Kennedy, Pat Moynihan and the then Governor of New York, Hugh Carey – who expressed their "deep hurt" at the transfer. Haughey and his Minister for Foreign Affairs Brian Lenihan backed down. Haughey later said there was no foundation to the reports that Sean Donlon was to be moved. The Department of Foreign Affairs reported that the transfer of Donlon was "totally without foundation" and that another diplomat, Noel Dorr, was being appointed to the UN post.

The American fund-raising committee, appointed by Haughey, was called the Friends of Fianna Fáil. At a later stage, they organised a fund-raiser for the ailing Tanaiste, Brian Lenihan, who urgently needed a liver transplant in a Pittsburgh Hospital. That money was raised in a few days following a phone call from Haughey.

The American dollar well was running dry and the fund raising committee was relatively inactive in the last few years of Mr. Haughey's leadership. Albert Reynolds totally revamped it, bringing in the well-respected senior Fianna Fáil figure, Eoin Ryan, to head it. The former Senator, who had influential business connections, had been on the Fianna Fáil committee during the time of the leadership of Jack Lynch, but when Haughey took over Ryan did not like the way the finances were organised and so he resigned. Under the leadership of trustee, Rich Howlin, a number of very successful golf classics were organised and these reaped a rich harvest for the Soldiers of Destiny. The debt was reduced to a manageable £500,000 before Taoiseach Bertie Ahern took over from Albert Reynolds.

19

EARLY ATTEMPTS AT PEACEMAKING

Haughey had contacts with Sinn Fein from the early 1980s, when the IRA hunger strikes probably scuppered his chances of winning the 1981 election. After 1987, he was aware of soundings by the Republican leadership about finding a way to end the IRA campaign.

But he never grasped the opportunity to begin a "peace process" in the way Albert Reynolds did. This seems to contrast with the boldness – some would have said foolhardiness – of many of his decisions that led to the establishment of the Financial Services Centre in Dublin's docklands.

Indeed, Haughey briefed Reynolds about the approaches before leaving office. He told him that if he wanted to make something of it, he might like to keep Haughey's Northern adviser, Martin Mansergh, on the team. (Such was Mansergh's central role, that even John Bruton tried to keep him on when he became Taoiseach, but Mansergh stayed loyal to Fianna Fáil). It was, apparently, about the only thing on which an embittered Haughey, who blamed Reynolds for his downfall, briefed the new Taoiseach. Reynolds not only kept the clever and immensely experienced Mansergh on board, but decided to make the ending of Northern violence a central policy of his administration. The Labour party claims that the briefing Dick Spring got on the prospects for peace was a key factor in its controversial decision to join forces with Fianna Fáil to form a government.

Insiders claim that things went a lot further under Haughey's government than has been generally acknowledged. They say the final draft of the Downing Street Declaration – the key document in the process towards the IRA cease-fire – was drafted by Mansergh during Haughey's time in 1991.

Could Haughey, then, have been the man to broker the cease-fire? Given time, perhaps he might. He did not know he was going to be ejected from office before what he would regard as his own good time. But he had good reason to be cautious. The events of the Arms Trial must have made him acutely sensitive to the dangers of getting involved in Northern affairs. Those same events made him a figure of huge suspicion to almost everyone outside Fianna Fáil. They gave him some standing with Republicans, but not much; their general attitude would have been that Haughey's heart might be in the right place, but that he was not to be trusted.

Haughey also had unparalleled experience. His ability to charm foreign leaders was remarkable, encompassing such an unlikely group as Francois Mitterand, Margaret Thatcher and Jacques Delors. Perhaps unwisely, he gave up on Mrs. Thatcher during the pressures of the hunger strike election, while the relationship with Mitterand seems to have been more of a mutual admiration society. But the friendship with Delors - described as "a real rapport" – was of significance. One can easily imagine that French style and the belief of the French elite in its fitness and right to govern, would have appealed to the admirer of Napoleon. The French, equally, would have found Haughey more congenial than the cold English or vulgar Americans. In any event, Reynolds also partly reaped where Haughey had sown, with Delors' support vital in securing for Ireland a doubling of EU structural funds.

But history has yet to deliver its final verdict on whether Haughey was right to move slowly on the peace process, and whether Reynolds's foot-to-the-floor approach forced the various parties into negotiations before they were really ready. Haughey judged that Sinn Fein was not ready when the first approaches came. His press secretary and friend Padraig O hAnnrachain had confidential discussions with Gerry Adams but the impetus came after the Enniskillen bombing, which one insider describes as a "traumatic shock" not just to the Haughey government but to many people in the Republican movement as well. The Redemptorist priest Fr Alex Reid, who has played a key role in the entire peace process arranged two meetings between O' hAnnrachain, Adams and other senior Sinn Fein people in a monastery in Dundalk. The contacts were made in great secrecy and even SDLP leader John Hume was probably unaware that these meetings were taking place. But the government representatives found that Sinn Fein seemed unaware of what would be required of them and especially of he IRA if they were to enter the political process. He gave this assessment to Haughey and the contacts were broken off.

It was not until 1991 that the situation seemed to have changed sufficiently for another attempt. Fr Reid again was a go-between for the Hume/Adams dialogue. Hume met Haughey and briefed him on the results of his meetings. Martin Mansergh was called in to put some of this down on paper. The result was a first draft of what became the Downing Street declaration and was known then as "Hume/Adams," although it would appear that the two party leaders did not draw up a formal document.

It was widely assumed at the time that Hume had given the government a document setting out their ideas for a peace process. But sources in the administration insist that Haughey, through Mansergh, was centrally involved in the drafting and that it contained the essence of the Downing Street Declaration. So far, the British had not been involved. Haughey briefly mentioned what was going on to Prime Minister John Major at an EU summit in 1991. Major was non-committal, but showed some interest. Again, it transpired later that the British were having their own contacts with Republicans, unbeknownst to the Irish.

Sinn Fein and Hume put pressure on Haughey to arrange a meeting with Adams. But, like Reynolds after him, he insisted there could be no such meeting until the IRA had called off its campaign. In fact, such a meeting would have been very premature. Haughey believed that, particularly with his record, he might have to resign if the story of the contacts broke. So, from his own point of view, he was taking a considerable risk for peace. He was more vulnerable than Reynolds, who carried no Northern baggage, so he moved very cautiously. Even those who worked with him at the time are unsure whether he believed that anything would come of the peace process.

There seems little doubt that Haughey cared about the North and he was fairly Republican in his outlook. At university, he was involved in leading a party of students to remove a Union Jack flying over Trinity College to mark Armistice Day. Some see his father's history as important in shaping Haughey's attitudes. He fought with the IRA in Co Derry in the War of Independence but joined Michael Collins's new Irish Army after the Treaty. It is interesting to note, as emerged years later, that while fighting the anti-Treaty IRA in the South, Collins was helping to arm the IRA in the North; ostensibly to fend off attacks against the Catholic community, but probably also because the final shape of post Treaty Ireland was far from decided at that point. Fianna Fáil, of course, emerged from the anti Treaty side and many of the party old guard were suspicious of Haughey's pro-Treaty family background. That part of Haughey's life might well have been easier had they known the full story. But the parallels with the attempted running of guns to the North in 1969/70 are striking, even though Haughey denied any knowledge of this and was acquitted in the Arms Trial.

Whatever he may have felt personally, his iron political discipline made him keep his distance in the early Sinn Fein contacts. Some close to the scene think he may have regretted this caution later, seeing what Reynolds achieved, but Sinn Fein's initial ideas were seen as wildly divorced from reality.

Adams seemed to think that it was possible to break Sinn Fein's political isolation even if the IRA campaign continued. He proposed a "pan-nationalist" front of political parties north and south to push for a political settlement, but did not include an IRA cease-fire in the plan. He believed there would be grassroots support within Fianna Fáil for such a plan. But Haughey's representatives were instructed to tell him that no Irish government could even appear to be involved in any alliance while the violence continued.

Haughey supporters claim Reynolds could not have brokered the IRA cease-fire without the work done under Haughey's government. They say the all-party talks now under way are essentially the same as the constitutional conference advocated consistently by Haughey. One difference, though, is that the talks are firmly in the context of the Northern Ireland state. Those who used to say at the time that only Haughey had the credentials to deliver a deal may have had a point. It is unlikely that any of his rivals as party leader would have struck such a nationalist tone. As such, the Provisionals might not have been willing to make the initial contacts that began the subsequent chain of events.

20

C J's POWERFUL BUSINESS FRIENDS

Dermot Desmond is the most remarkable of Haughey's business friends and associates. He is also different from the others, both in terms of the relationship and the kind of businessman he is. The others tended, in one way or the other, to be part of Haughey's circle. They were accountants, like Des Traynor, or property developers, like John Byrne. Desmond seems genuinely to have admired Haughey's abilities, and particularly his determination to get things done. Perhaps, like the late Joe Moore, founder of the PMPA insurance company, he also admired Haughey's brand of nationalism.

Talent, and the ability to get things done, are certainly Desmond hallmarks. As the son of a customs officer, (who ironically, was stationed at Dublin airport during the attempt to import arms for which Haughey later stood trial and was acquitted) Desmond did not have any automatic entree into the world of finance. But after a spell working in the World Bank, Desmond decided that was what he was going to do. He did not like the fact that stockbroking in Dublin was dominated by a handful of firms, most of them associated with old Protestant money. He founded National City Brokers (NCB) as a money-broker – someone that essentially shaves fractions off the cost of money for clients. This was a business where skill and ingenuity were more important that the personal connections that dominated conventional stockbroking.

Soon NCB was sufficiently successful to move on into share

and bond dealing and to rank eventually as one of the "Big Four" firms with Davys, Riada and Goodbodys. It was a remarkable achievement to come from nowhere in a business where many of the firms were founded in the last century. Along the way, he showed much of the original vision that has characterised most of his investment decisions. He was not content just to have NCB buy the fancy computer equipment central to modern financial dealing. He spun off a successful company that designed software for the industry. He was also an early investor in Irish cream liqueurs - one of great marketing success stories of modern times.

However, Desmond's really big idea at least as far as the public is concerned, was the International Financial Services Centre (IFSC) in Dublin's docklands. When he put forward his plan, it was the mid eighties, a time of stock market boom when the City of London was bursting at the seams and short of people and services like telecommunications. The idea of re-developing derelict docklands had already been established in cities like Boston, so Desmond got the idea of putting the two together and setting up a financial centre in Dublin's redundant docks? Dublin had much to offer – an English-speaking workforce and advanced telecommunications – as an alternative to London. The other great attraction for Dublin was Ireland's tried and tested industrial incentive – the 10pc corporation tax on profits. This was revolutionary. It was one thing to offer the tax to the offshoots of multi-national manufacturers, quite another to extend it to the hugely profitable financial services industry. It was rather too much for Fine Gael leader Garret FitzGerald, to whom the idea was first proposed. He had earmarked docks for development in the early 1980s, but could see no way that the tax breaks could be ring-fenced only for foreign activities. It was, however, the kind of jobs that were needed for Dublin and there was the biggest piece of property development in the history of the State. Even better, the State would be largely in control of the process, because it was State-owned land and the tenants would have to be approved and licensed to qualify for the lower tax. Haughey went about the plan with extraordinary gusto, taking almost personal charge of the scheme and bringing it to fruition in a matter of months. Desmond was one of the major investors, with a stake in one of the office blocks in the centre. There was a hairy period, when the 1987 stock market crash scuppered the original concept of taking the overload from the City in London. The IFSC moved instead towards attracting fund management and administrative functions for investment institutions and insurance companies. Desmond had to carry a lot of costs while he looked for tenants for his block, before Ulster Bank moved in.

The IFSC has since become a very successful venture for its investors. Desmond was able to enjoy prime rents on his property before selling it to Ulster Bank and embarking on a series of original investments including Glasgow Celtic football club and London's City Airport.

Haughey and Desmond remained close, with the financier a source of valued advice. The relationship survived the Telecom scandal when Desmond felt obliged to step down as chairman of Aer Rianta after a political dispute over his role in the purchase of a Ballsbridge site from Telecom Eireann and its subsequent resale at a huge profit.

There were claims in the court proceedings surrounding the takeover battle for whiskey company Irish Distillers - denied by Desmond - that he had been able to phone Haughey to clarify what the tax treatment would be for Distillers' shareholders.

The McCracken Tribunal was told that Desmond had paid almost £500,000 in investments, loans and gifts to Haughey's children, or companies with which they were associated. This included a £75,000 loan for the refurbishment of Haughey's yacht, Celtic Mist, in consultation with Haughey's son Conor; a £275,000 investment in Conor's mining company, Feltrim; and a commercial advance of £100,000 to Ciaran Haughey's Celtic Helicopters. But Desmond stressed that he had never made any donations to Haughey while he was in active politics. He confirmed that he had made payments to Haughey since he left office in 1994 and there have been regular rumours that Desmond has been willing to bail Haughey out of financial disaster, if that should turn out to be his final state. Others may have given money in hope of favours, but Desmond may well have been a genuine supporter and admirer of Haughey's style.

—-oOo—-

If there is a pattern to the kind of businessman who became associated with Haughey, Robert Pino Harris fits the bill perfectly. He is from Dublin's Northside, a self-made millionaire many times over, and he shuns the limelight. Harris, in fact, carries all these qualities to extremes. His father was a horse-dealer, originally from Limerick, who set up a scrap business in Dublin not long after Pino was born. Young Robert had little interest in school and left it early to go into the family business. Neighbours recall him collecting scrap from a pony and cart. But Harris – a man who lives for work – was clearly ambitious. He acquired the rights to assemble Guy trucks, then a leading brand, in Ireland. But he lost out when Guy was absorbed into British Leyland and the Irish franchise went to the Leyland dealer. One story has it that the Leyland representative told Harris quite firmly that Guy had no place for him in Ireland, to which Harris replied that there would be no place for Guy trucks in Ireland.

Harris went to the Geneva Motor Show, and liked the design and power of a new Japanese truck, the Hino, so much that he waited around for three days to meet the Hino representatives, who were very impressed by the fact that he wanted to purchase 300 trucks. He could not afford all these vehicles for he didn't have that kind of money, but he also knew that Hino didn't have enough vehicles to fill such a huge order. Harris gradually built up his imports and started exporting them to England, eventually blitzing the British market with his powerful Japanese Hino franchise. He took on the British in their own backyard by assembling Hinos in Liverpool in the 1980s and defeated legal attempts by other truck manufacturers to stop him, claiming that he was using illegal means to get around import restrictions on Japanese vehicles. Harris is a born salesman, with an eye for human psychology he may have inherited from his father's horse-dealing days. Early Japanese trucks, like their cars, were much better equipped than European rivals. Harris concentrated on drivers as much as the fleet-buyers to create interest, pointing out how much better the Hinos were equipped for the comfort of the man behind the wheel. "He operates a kind of reverse marketing psychology," one associate recalled, "saying if you don't want it, there's plenty of others who do."

His lack of education apparently shows when it comes to

reading and writing but not where figures are concerned. Put a calculator in his hand and show him a balance sheet and he is in his element. Apart from a fondness for fancy cars - he has owned several Rolls-Royces and Bentleys, as well as top-of-the-range Mercedes - business seems to be major interest. "His manner is rough and abrasive. He is a dour and sullen person who comes alive when he is doing business," was how one associate described him. It is this dour disposition and reclusive lifestyle that have made him such a source of fascination. He does not inhabit the jet-setting world of bloodstock, high-stakes golf tournaments and luxury foreign homes of Dermot Desmond or Michael Smurfit. Instead, he chose to live in a converted terrace house in inner city Dublin with his elderly mother, who apparently was not at all happy when they moved to a mansion in Ashbourne, Co Meath, and insisted on returning to the family home in Phibsboro. So he bought the adjoining terrace house and knocked it down to provide his mother and himself with a bit more space.

Legend has it that he abandoned a foreign holiday after only a few days because of his commitment to business. Driving holidays in Ireland are regularly interrupted by visits to Hino dealers. Even in the business world, he keeps to himself. Although he has added the Isuzu and Iveco franchises to his empire, he is not a member of the trade body, the Society of Irish Motor Importers. The business has been kept very much in the family too, with his brother Gerry and half-brother Billy (by his mother's first marriage) working in the firm. His long-time partner, Denise, is also an employee of the firm.

Harris was not known to have a close relationship with Haughey, or having much interest in politics. But Haughey would have been well aware of him, for he was one of the biggest employers in Haughey's constituency. Harris has supplied trucks for Fianna Fáil election campaigns, including Sean Haughey's attempt to win a Dail seat. He had a brush with the politicians in a row over 150 acres of land he owned in Santry Woods demesne. In 1982, Fianna Fáil councillors supported re-zoning the land for industrial use, but this was rescinded after local protests.

21

✿

GREAT ACHIEVER OR GRAND ILLUSIONIST

Nothing that has been revealed so far has dented the belief of many people that Haughey was a great political leader, whose achievements far outweigh any harm he may have done. Of these, the greatest is undoubtedly the restoration of the government finances after 1987. But this is not what most ordinary people remember him by. Rather it is a series of small actions, which were very important to those who benefited from them.

Haughey himself believed in the power of inexpensive but imaginative gestures, and his instinct was undoubtedly sound. The most effective was probably the introduction of free travel on public transport and free TV licences for old-age pensioners in 1967. This costs very little although that may change as the population ages. But it is still talked about, more than thirty years after its introduction, and almost everyone seems to know that Haughey brought it in. The scheme, along with the later introduction of free telephone rental, is also the envy of pensioners' organisations in other countries.

Haughey also set considerable store by his record on women's rights. As Minister for Justice, he brought in the legislation that gave women equal rights to their husbands under the inheritance laws. He was involved in the setting-up of the Commission on the Status of Women and his appointment of Maire Geoghegan-Quinn to his Cabinet in 1979 made her the first Irish government Minister since Countess Markievicz, appointed at the foundation of the state. He was the Minister who introduced the farmers dole, which gave a minimum income to the poorest small farmers – before there was any EU money available.

His classic low-cost, imaginative gesture was perhaps the granting of tax-free status to creative artists. Few Irish ones earned enough to be significant taxpayers anyway, and the measure persuaded some wealthy foreign writers and filmmakers to live in Ireland. It also fitted nicely with Haughey's image of himself as a Renaissance-style patron of the arts. He set up the Aosdana scheme in 1982, which he may have seen as an embryo Academe Francaise. It is a group of 150 self-chosen artists who are entitled to grants from the State. In that year, too, he abolished VAT on books. He also appreciated, in a way which few other politicians, or civil servants, seemed to, the value of Dublin's historic buildings and the need to preserve them. The restoration of the Royal Hospital at Kilmainham, and the sale of the Georgian houses in Merrion Street for restoration as part of the luxury Merrion Hotel are down to him. So too is the refurbishment of Government Buildings and its use for the purpose which, it is believed, the British secretly intended it when it was built during the agitation for Home Rule. His use of Irish artists and craftworkers in the building was in stark contrast to the kind of austerity associated with Irish public buildings.

To the"begrudgers" these gestures, however worthy, were also part and parcel of Haughey's failings, and why they thought he was not to be trusted with power. His attitude of getting something done (whatever the political and legal niceties) without worrying about cost, could be fine when doing something small and imaginative, but dangerous on the bigger stage.

The provision of free hospital care for all may have been part of Fianna Fáil's policy after the 1977 election, but appeared not to have been costed. Haughey had more support for his controls on tobacco advertising. He also showed considerable courage and skill in getting through the first legalisation on contraceptives, even if he may have come to regret his description of the carefully hedged provisions as "an Irish solution to an Irish problem". What is certain is that Haughey was one of the few Ministers for

Health to leave that job with his political reputation enhanced, rather than damaged. It seems likely that Jack Lynch gave him the job when he was forced to take him back into the Cabinet on the grounds that Haughey could do himself little good there and might come to grief. Not for the first or last time, he had been under-estimated.

Haughey is also given credit for the re-generation of much of the city of Dublin, in both the International Financial Services Centre (IFSC) and Temple Bar. Both were projects likely to appeal to him, as they in effect turned the State into a property developer. Haughey, like many in Fianna Fáil, maintained that the number of construction cranes on the skyline was a mark of economic well being. His friend and supporter, the financier Dermot Desmond, was a strong proponent of the idea of building a financial centre on Dublin's derelict docklands and promoting it with generous tax rates. Garret FitzGerald, as Taoiseach, worried about how the tax incentives could be confined to foreign institutions and did not move on the plan. He was right in thinking that the IFSC could not be completely ring-fenced for foreigners but Haughey had no qualms about that. He exerted the full force of his powers of command to get the scheme moving in double quick time. It offered the prospect of substantial immediate construction jobs and the long-term revitalisation of rundown areas.

The IFSC has been a great success, although not quite in the way originally envisaged. At the time, the City of London was bursting at the seams after the "Big Bang" deregulation. People hoped that dealing rooms would move to Dublin, but the Crash of 1987 put paid to that. Instead, the IFSC has become a centre for "back-office" administrative operations and the management of investment funds. That enables huge amounts of profits to be recorded through Dublin by the foreign institutions, at only 10% tax. So much so that the IFSC has been a source of great concern and annoyance to many of Ireland's European partners. Successive governments have defended it strongly, and no wonder. Over 2,000 people are employed directly in the centre, and perhaps as many again in spin-off jobs. There are no official figures for the tax take from the IFSC, but, even at 10%, it is reckoned to be at least £500 million a year.

Yet the revelations about the funding of Haughey's lifestyle inevitably raise questions about his motivations for such schemes. The IFSC looked like a guaranteed money-spinner for the developers and investors. Firms wishing to locate in the IFSC had to have a licence, and they had to locate in the centre. Investors in the buildings - including Desmond - had a closed rental market, where rents were up to double the levels in other parts of the city. In fact, the centre's slow start gave them quite a fright and developing and letting the buildings took longer than planned. It was quite a few years before real money was made. It is also true that successive governments have proved just as generous as Haughey with taxpayers' money in the centre, and with less justification, now that it is a proven success.

Temple Bar has also been something of a disappointment, for different reasons. The idea was to set up a State company to develop the area and rent or sell the properties to investors. There would be a sweetener through tax breaks. What seems to have gone wrong is a concentration on maximising investors' profits, so that the area was swamped with pubs and hotels and in danger of becoming just a large-scale drinking den. There is also plenty of evidence that a preponderance of investors have links to Fianna Fáil. Much of the damage has been done since Haughey left office and it is possible that his vision for the area would have been broader. He could well argue that securing benefits for the state, while giving the opportunity to make profits to friends and supporters, is a win-win game. There would have been a lot of force to that argument, were it not for the discovery of the Ansbacher accounts that cast doubt on all his motives and actions.

When Haughey became Taoiseach many people, whatever else they thought about him, believed he was the right person to fix the economy. They argued that somebody with such a successful business career would know how to deal with the national finances as well. We now know that Haughey's business success was largely an illusion. Yet it is clear that he did know what needed to be done when he came into power. His 1980 television speech, in which he said the country was living beyond its means and action would have to be taken to reduce government borrowing, is still remembered. Yet Haughey ducked the challenge. Opponents say this was because he was afraid to court unpopularity and was willing to flirt with national bankruptcy to stay in power or regain it. Supporters believe it was politically impossible to deliver the necessary spending cuts and higher taxes in the circumstances of the time.

Insiders say Haughey had a plan, which involved holding an election in March 1981. After that, the pruning sheers would be wielded. In the meantime, an easy Budget would be brought in January so as not to frighten the electorate. Part of this plan was the appointment of Gene Fitzgerald as Minister for Finance. The Cork TD knew little about finance and was certainly not one to stand up to Haughey. The real difficulty was that the budgetary figures would not allow for any planned reduction in borrowing unless there was a harsh Budget. Opponents within Fianna Fáil claim, and leaked documents tend to verify, that Haughey over-ruled Department of Finance officials in order to get lower spending estimates which would allow him to square the circle. The official estimates for government spending were arbitrarily cut by £115 million, with no changes in policy to explain where the savings would be made. Another £100 million of capital spending was handed over to the private sector to finance, even though no such arrangements were in place. There was consternation in the Department but nobody resigned. Some senior politicians who were horrified by Haughey's action believe the civil servants should have prepared a memorandum for the next government, headed by Garret FitzGerald, to show what had happened, but they didn't.

The significance of the claims is that they show the lengths to which Haughey would go, and his apparent disregard for the normal conventions of government. But while his behaviour may have been reprehensible, there was a certain justification for his political plans. He had inherited a mess from Jack Lynch. The architects of his economic policy, George Colley and Martin O'Donoghue, were among Haughey's most implacable opponents. They had failed to take action on government borrowing, especially after the oil price crisis of 1979. Why should Haughey risk losing everything he had fought so hard to achieve, because of his enemies' mistakes? There is evidence, though, that Haughey intended only getting the election out of the way and had little notion of tackling the economic problems seriously. For a start, Haughey announced that Departmental spending cuts would be discussed bilaterally between Ministers and Gene Fitzgerald, rather than at Cabinet level. One senior Minister recalls going in to see the Finance Minister to find Haughey sitting beside him. The Taoiseach did nearly all the talking. The particular Minister claims that Haughey said he would have to cut his departmental budget by £20 million, but this would be restored after the election by way of supplementary estimates in the Dáil. When the Minister queried this irregular procedure, Haughey got angry and said, "What the fuck is wrong with you?"

But things went wrong with the plan. The tragic fire at the Stardust disco in Dublin on St Valentine's night put paid to the scheme for a snap March election. In the meantime, the populist measures introduced to help win the election were running away with the public finances. They included government departments and state companies being virtually ordered to hire more staff whether they needed them or not. Public sector pay claims were settled on any terms the workers wanted, so that average public sector earnings rose by almost 30 per cent in 1980. By the time the election finally was held in June, the hunger strike by IRA prisoners in the Maze was well under way. The success of two absentionist IRA candidates in border constituencies deprived Haughey of the chance of tying the combined Fine Gael/Labour representation and retaining office. With hindsight it might be argued that the voters were already looking for financial rectitude from government. Haughey may have been unlucky but continuing with the borrowing did not buy him popularity. Government debt was already a major media issue and a tighter policy might have brought better political results.

Haughey had been a model Finance Minister in the 1960s, bringing in the last balanced Budget before the present sequence in the late 1990s. He criticised Lynch's 1976 Fianna Fáil manifesto with its promise to abolish domestic rates and car tax and spend the country to economic success. Ironically, he was one of the main political beneficiaries of those policies. Haughey was Minister for Health and much of the extra money was spent on the health service, with thousands of extra staff employed. As

149

Taoiseach, Haughey applied more of the same medicine, demanding increases in employment in state companies and government services in an attempt to keep unemployment down. Jack Lynch's earlier pledge that Fianna Fáil deserved to lose the election if unemployment went above 100,000 was a millstone round Haughey's neck.

He got another chance to see if he could do better sooner than anyone would have predicted. After his defeat in the June election, he did not seem to know what to do in opposition, taking weeks to appoint a front bench team. He only began to move when it dawned on him that FitzGerald's minority government might not last and power could possibly be regained. Evidence that Haughey intended a different tack came with the offer of a post to Martin O'Donoghue. Although associated with the 1976 manifesto, O'Donoghue now argued for fiscal correction. He was surprised by the approach, and especially an offer to resurrect his abolished Ministry of Economic Planning and Development. That seemed unlikely to be credible and there was still the problem of what policy was actually going to be.

"What's the problem?" asked Haughey, when O'Donoghue raised this. "You're for growth and employment and I'm for growth and employment."

O'Donoghue was appointed Finance spokesman, less than two weeks before the Fine Gael/Labour coalition was due to bring in a Budget. The issue was what attitude should Fianna Fáil take to the Budget? Haughey's instincts were that one could hardly expect to win an election donning the government hairshirt but O'Donoghue and others argued that calling for more spending and borrowing would be both irresponsible and politically damaging. Eventually it was agreed that Fianna Fáil would accept the government's budgetary targets but argue about the details of how they were to be achieved. The minority government fell when the coalition failed to persuade socialist TD Jim Kemmy to support the imposition of VAT on children's clothes and shoes. Suddenly, it was an election campaign, and Haughey's old instincts re-asserted themselves.

At a press conference, Haughey was unable to bring himself to keep to the agreed line of accepting the coalition targets, with the clear implication that Fianna Fáil would also have to cut spending and/or raise taxes somewhere else. Instead, he said people should not be hypnotised by government borrowing – then running at a billion pounds a year. At a stormy emergency front bench meeting next day, senior party figures, including deputy leader George Colley, Des O'Malley and O'Donoghue, made clear they would not campaign unless the line were held.

Haughey did not want to lay it on the line himself. "You're the Finance spokesman; you make a speech on it," he said to O'Donoghue. But his critics insisted and in the end O'Donoghue drafted a speech which was issued to the media under Haughey's name.

Fianna Fáil came up with a plan to meet the coalitions target of keeping borrowing to £715m by applying VAT to imports at the point of entry and the accelerated collection of business taxes. These were one-off measures, which could not deal with the real problems. Even so, on the hustings, Haughey could not resist making promises to various interest groups. The classic moment was over whether Fianna Fáil would continue to support the controversial regional airport at Knock, Co Mayo. When O'Donoghue was asked at a front bench press conference if he supported the project, Haughey was heard to hiss: "Say yes." Instead, O'Donoghue said no, while adding that he thought government commitments should be met.

Evidence that people wanted the public finances corrected comes from the fact that there was no collapse in support for the coalition despite the harsh Budget and the debacle over failing to get it through. Instead, Fianna Fáil gained only 2pc of the vote over the previous election, and half of that was the return of voters who had previously supported the hunger strike candidates. Haughey was two short of a majority and three Workers Party TDs and four Independents held the balance of power. For those who argued that the public actually wanted the Haughey of the 1980 TV broadcast, the proof was a huge vote for Charlie McCreevy, who had to resign earlier from the parliamentary party for criticising economic policy.

Before he could do anything, Haughey had to get back into power. The "Gregory deal," which he negotiated with Independent TD Tony Gregory, is often cited as Haughey at his worst, squandering public money for political gain. However, Garret FitzGerald was making similar offers. The projects were largely admirable, although the same needs could have been identified elsewhere. More significant, perhaps, was Haughey's comment that Gregory was "pushing an open door," and the fact that the cost of the plan hardly seemed to matter to him. Where office was at stake, Haughey's negotiating stance often seemed to be to give whatever was asked for. FitzGerald, on the other hand, presented Gregory with a plan he had drawn up, and his priorities were different from Gregory's. FitzGerald was concerned both about cost, and fairness to the rest of the country. The deal seemed to indicate Haughey's penchant for flying by the seat of his pants. It was hugely expensive, and ideas such as the nationalisation of the loss-making Clondalkin Paper Mills would have long-term cost implications. It is hard to square them with the ostensible objective of reducing government deficits. Supporters of Haughey say politics is like that and three elections in less than two years was bound to strain things. "The line always bends when an election is looming," said one close adviser. "The best thing for the economy is when the government falls unexpectedly within a week." Haughey may have been playing both ends against the middle. In a surprise move, he appointed Ray MacSharry Minister for Finance. MacSharry had supported Haughey in the various leadership challenges but he was no Gene Fitzgerald. Nor was he one of those who was cowed by Haughey's presence. If Haughey had planned to ride roughshod over the public finances again, he would hardly have picked MacSharry.

Neither Fitzgerald nor Michael O'Kennedy as Finance Minister had been able to face Haughey down. Some Ministers would check anxiously with officials before going into Cabinet meetings to see what sort of mood "the Boss" was in. Many officials could not face him down either, although Maurice Doyle, Secretary of the Dept of Finance and later Governor of the Central Bank, was one who could. MacSharry, perhaps because of his position, does not recall Haughey as having a particularly autocratic style. He would say his piece and, as he saw it, other Ministers would do the same.

The new Haughey government started off, though, much as

the old one had ended. In fairness, in those days most Irish politicians and commentators were imbued with crypto-Keynsian ideas that governments could spend their way out of recession. And, of course, the government was still in a minority. There is also the fact that it was assumed that spending cuts and tax rises would send the country deeper into recession. And so they probably would have, in the circumstances of the time. Aides say Haughey favoured action on the spending side rather than tax hikes. These would probably have done less damage than the tax rises from the later Fine Gael/Labour coalition, when Dick Spring vetoed deep spending cuts.

MacSharry put a new phrase into the national vocabulary when he promised to replace the "gloom and doom" of the coalition with "boom and bloom." It was quite a hostage to fortune, given the state of the public finances at the time. And they were to worsen even further under the pressure of by-elections, as Haughey rowed back even on the limited correction in the 1982 Budget. Higher PRSI rates announced at Budget time were later offset by an increase in tax allowances. More dangerous, and more typical of Haughey's style at the time, was the offer of Exchequer-subsidised loans and tax breaks to home buyers to head off a rise in mortgage rates.

It was this period that carved out the image of Haughey as someone who would take any risk with the economy for the sake of popularity and electoral success. One who worked with him at the time said his attitude was a mixture of believing you could spend your way out of recession and wanting to be popular. Supporters say this was not an unreasonable attitude in the context of the times. In a cleverly oblique speech at Listowel Writers Week in 1996, Fianna Fáil's Anglo-Irish adviser, Dr Martin Mansergh, said; "Society is full of conflicting and contradictory interests and aspirations. The art of politics is to reconcile them without too much friction, while propelling society as a whole forward." It is worth noting, for example, that it was the Labour Party that proposed the state take-over of the failed Fieldcrest towelling factory in Kilkenny. No surprise in that, perhaps, but Fine Gael added the demand that this be done before the year was out!

Yet, whatever the political situation, by mid-1982, it was clear that something would have to be done. MacSharry confided later that he could not sleep at night worrying about the country's indebtedness. Little did he know it would have doubled by the time he was Finance Minister again. He believes that it took more courage to propose corrective action in 1982 than it did in 1987. Economic conditions were more hostile and the government more vulnerable, depending essentially on left-wing TDs for support. On the other hand, the situation was now critical. The borrowing target of £679m had been reached by the middle of the year and looked like it might reach £1bn for the year as whole. Haughey suggested that the government would have to review the situation and draw up new targets for the rest of the year. An economic sub-committee was formed and MacSharry faced down Workers Party demands for more spending. The July "mini-budget" proposed cuts of £120m in government spending for the rest of the year. A public service pay rise was postponed, special pay rises were frozen and food subsidies were reduced. Not everyone was convinced the numbers added up, but MacSharry claims they were the biggest cutbacks ever contained in a supplementary estimate and is still sore that Fianna Fáil got no credit for it from opposition or media.

In an attempt to give the government more to sell than just spending cuts, Padraig O hUiginn, the grey eminence who presided as Secretary of the Taoiseach's Department, took time off to prepare a document called, "The Way Forward." The Dept of Finance was furious at this encroachment on their turf but the plan was launched with great fanfare as the blueprint for the future. The great issue of the time was the current budget deficit – the gap between tax revenues and day-to-day government spending and debt servicing. The plan promised to eliminate this by 1986 through spending cuts and economic growth of 5pc a year – ambitious by any standards. With hindsight and as Garret FitzGerald found out, economic conditions in the mid-1980s would not have allowed it. As it was, the plan spelt the end of the minority government. The Workers Party would not support the new thrust of policy, with its emphasis on spending cuts. Although Haughey tried several stratagems to stave off defeat, including an approach to the Labour party and bringing the ill TD Jim Gibbons to the Dáil in an ambulance, there was no attempt to go back on the economic plan and the government was defeated in a Dáil vote.

Four years later, Haughey was back in power. The economy and public finances were in even worse shape and there were very few who thought he was the man to put them right. The coalition had collapsed in bizarre circumstances, with Fine Gael introducing the tough Budget it said was needed but which its Labour partners would not countenance. Fianna Fáil campaigned shamelessly against the Budget measures, targeting the effects of health cutbacks on the sick and elderly. Again, the tactic failed. Even in these circumstances, Haughey failed to win a majority. There was much talk of the "Haughey factor," but how much of that was a perception that he could not be trusted with the public finances?

Almost everyone had missed the significance of the shift in 1982. Instead of another spree, Haughey and MacSharry resumed where they had left off in correcting the public finances. This time, luck was on their side. Election pledges were ruthlessly ditched. But then, as Mansergh said in that speech, quoting Machiavelli, "Consistency is the hobgoblin of small minds." He recalls Haughey reprimanding a front bench spokesperson for repeating an election promise a few days after the election had been won.

Finding the required savings was no easy matter. Financier Dermot Desmond had influenced Haughey during the spell in opposition. As well as advocating what became the International Financial Services Centre, Desmond had stressed the need for budgetary correction. His ideas centred on cuts in social welfare and most insiders thought that was where the axe would fall heaviest. Instead, it was Health that bore the brunt, as in 1982. It was politically easier, and it was also the area Haughey knew best, from his time as Minister. But there was no alternative to crushing detail if the job was to be done. Every subhead and vote from every Department was examined for possible cuts, and then examined again and again. One of the strangest images of that time is of MacSharry and Department Secretary Sean Cromien in their offices late at night, huddled in their overcoats against the cold. The bureaucratic machine was unable to provide heating after office hours as they went over the endless detail of spending plans.

Spending Ministers and their officials argued, of course, that the cuts were impossible. Haughey's determination was crucial. When the arguments got bogged down, he would say to MacSharry, "What do you think. Ray?" If MacSharry said, as he usually did, that the money had to be saved further savings would be made. Cuts of as little as £500 were identified and implemented. Cromien and the newly appointed Governor of the Central Bank, Maurice Doyle, met constantly to review the situation.

Murray was crucial to one of the key elements of the programme – a voluntary redundancy package for the public service. This was also Haughey's idea and nothing like it had ever been tried before. Public servants were entitled to jobs for life. Although there was no suggestion of compulsory redundancies, unions might still have balked at conceding the principle even of voluntary ones. Haughey got round this by making the terms so generous that, as one trade union leader put it, "We would have been killed in the rush if we'd tried to stand in their way." It was also important to get more senior, higher-earning staff to take redundancy so the package had to be attractive. Perhaps an even greater coup was getting the Central Bank to lend the government the money - in effect switching on the printing press – to cover the costs of the redundancy payments. In 1980, the Bank had refused to lend Haughey's government £350m, at the time Haughey was riding roughshod over the Dept of Finance.

This time, there were identifiable savings from the scheme and a government promise to repay from future Bank profits which would be due to the Exchequer. The fact that the Bank insisted on repayment confirmed Haughey's dislike and suspicion of the Bank. He felt it was far too conservative and held far more assets than was necessary – assets that could have been used by the government. The scheme raised some eyebrows, and the redundant workers' pensions had still to be paid for in the future, but it bought valuable time.

The other vital part of the package was a pay agreement with the unions. Haughey saw this, not just as a public sector pay deal to take the pressure off the government finances, but a general moderate deal to restore consumer and investor confidence. Trade Union leaders at the time believed Haughey was the only politician who could have pulled it off. He saw that spending cuts would not be enough without a return of confidence and investment. Not long after taking office, he invited the union leaders to meet him privately in his office. There was no soft-soaping; they had to wait some time in the corridor outside while Haughey finished his previous business.

When they went in, they found Haughey at his most gracious and charming, but also in his most commanding manner. He outlined the country's difficulties and how he intended to sort them out. The union bosses, well used to reading between the lines, got the message clearly. Haughey would sort it out with or without them. "The message was, "I'll do it without you if you don't come with me," one union leader recalls. "He didn't say that in so many words but it was clear that's what he meant."

The union leaders, who included the ICTU secretary Peter Cassells and the leaders of the major general and public service unions, were also given the unpalatable message that drastic spending cuts were coming. But the unions were in a weak position to argue. Unemployment and emigration were at record levels. Employers were largely ignoring the unions because the fear of job losses was enough to restrain wage demands. In the public sector; local authority workers were on half-time working because of shortage of funds. Their only demand at that time was that the pain would be evenly spread.

"We've got to swallow our spit and go along with this or he'll just roll over us," one of the union leaders said to his colleagues afterwards. So began what some say were the toughest negotiations of their careers to conclude a three-year national pay agreement with a pay pause and low increases thereafter. These were largely conducted by Padraig O hUiginn, now back in his accustomed place as the power behind the throne, having been sidelined while Garret FitzGerald was Taoiseach. O hUiginn spoke the trade unions' language, in that he believed in growth and expansion, and a powerful role for the State in delivering it. Both he and Haughey despised what they saw as the conservative number crunching of the Dept of Finance. But there was no question of expansion now, because of the state of the public finances. After three weeks hard bargaining, O hUiginn was insisting that three per cent, spread over three years was all that could be afforded. It was a lot of spit to swallow.

The unions tried to claw something back by way of a one-hour cut in the working week. But the employers would not play ball. They had only limited interest in a national deal anyway, believing they could do as well, in the circumstances, under free bargaining at company level. The talks were stalled. Now Haughey, who had not taken a direct part in them, moved again, in characteristic fashion. He phoned some of the most powerful employers in the country in the middle of the night and summoned them to Government Buildings, where negotiations were still going on. Haughey berated them for being short-sighted about where their own best interest lay and for their failure to act in the national interest, in blue language such as only Haughey could use. "You're acting the bollix over a lousy fucking one hour off the working week," was one quote.

The first the trade unions knew about this was when they spotted a group of sheepish-looking captains of industry in the corridor at 3am. The trick worked. In the view of one participant, Haughey, with his unrivalled feel for where power really resides, targetted the big companies. The unions got their shorter week and Haughey got his modest pay deal.

The final part of the plan was the blitz on the health services, of which the most notable was the closure of Barrington's hospital in Limerick. It was Haughey's one great act of political courage although he had always, in theory, favoured spending cuts over tax increases as the best way to correct the public finances. In coalition with Labour, FitzGerald had been forced to go the other way, savaging the private sector economy with tax rises, while leaving the public sector virtually unscathed. After Labour left the coalition, forcing an election, Fine Gael, drew up budgetary plans for cuts of around £200 million. This was more or less the final saving achieved by Fianna Fáil. The new Fine Gael leader, Alan Dukes, bravely supported the Haughey minority government in getting them through. But he was not alone. The late Frank Cluskey, a former Labour leader, hated Haughey with a passion. But he told colleagues he would break ranks if necessary, and go into the voting lobby with Fianna Fáil, to help get the measures through.

Even so, the programme might still have failed had it not coincided with falling international interest rates. To this was added a rapid fall in Irish rates as markets reacted to the improvements in the budgetary position. The boost to the economy, and the extra money in the pockets of borrowers, especially mortgage-holders, offset the effects of the cuts. Homeowners found their net income increasing by up to £15 a week over the following two years. But by 1989, the fat was gone and the cuts were affecting the real level of public services, especially health, so the gains on interest rates were crucial in protecting people's incomes and government services. For once Haughey had held his nerve and trusted his luck and, perhaps for the only time in his career, he got the big issue right.

22

THINGS THAT GO THUMP IN THE NIGHT

A long-standing relationship with Terry Keane was not Mr. Haughey's only amorous diversion during his years in power. However whatever indiscretion he might have been guilty of with the ladies, paled in comparison with the other events that surrounded his life.

There was a major crisis in the country during April 1970 when an attempt was made to import arms for the IRA in the North of Ireland, and allegations that Government Ministers were implicated.

On April 20, Taoiseach Jack Lynch revealed that he heard for the first time of the plot to import arms into this country (though the late Jim Gibbons, then Minister for Defence, was adamant later that he informed Mr. Lynch about the plot the previous November). Then just two days later, amid all sorts of rumours about the arms, the Dáil was informed that Mr. Haughey, due to deliver his budget speech in the Dáil that afternoon, had taken a bad fall from a horse in the grounds of his home in Kinsealy that morning and was in the Mater Private Hospital. Mr. Lynch, who had to deputise for Mr. Haughey and deliver his budget speech, only learned of the accident at lunchtime. And over the next few days, his mind was preoccupied with sensational information he had received about the arms importation from security sources.

While Mr. Haughey was recuperating in the Mater Hospital, the Taoiseach visited him. On Wednesday, April 29th, Mr. Lynch asked Haughey for his resignation for alleged involvement in illegal importation of arms. Lynch said later that Haughey was unable to speak at the time and needed time to consider his position. On Thursday April 30th veteran journalist Ned Murphy, political correspondent of the *Sunday Independent*, typed a story for submission to his editor, Hector Legge. The sensational story read:

"Whatever happened to the consignment of automatic weapons shipped to this country by air from Vienna on April 17th?

"Who gave permission for their entry to this country and why? Why was that permission cancelled after the advice notes had been received in Dublin? Who are the two gentlemen, very closely connected in Cabinet circles, who organised the gun running?

"Who was the departmental secretary who went to the highest authority in the land to ensure that the guns would not be landed?

"Why were previous warnings to the Government by Britain's M.I.5 about the previous activities of the organisers ignored?

"These are questions that must be answered if a certain story circulating only in the highest Government and official circles last week is to be proved untrue.A formal denial from the Government Information Bureau will not be enough. Evidence must be produced that a certain charter pilot had to be persuaded to take the weapons aboard in Vienna; that permission was given for their landing in Dublin; that the fact became known to the highest officers in the Garda and that it was only then that preventive action was taken to stop the landing."

The late Ned Murphy, who had the best policy and political contacts of any journalist at that time, regularly broke major stories since his arrival in Middle Abbey Street in the late twenties, including the declaration of the Irish Republic by the then Taoiseach of the Coalition Government, John A Costello, in Canada in 1949. But one of his best exclusives was the Connie Green story in 1955. Green, a member of the Saor Uladh organisation, was fatally shot in a raid on Roslea, Co Fermanagh, RUC barracks and was carried away by his comrades to die in a farmhouse just south of the Border. The Coalition Government agreed to a secret inquest (for which only 5 jurors could be found). It was held on a Saturday evening in a farmhouse with a Garda superintendent and detective sergeant as witnesses, while outside armed men awaited the remains for a midnight secret burial. The verdict was one of "death from gunshot wounds" on "an unknown man". The Dublin Government tried to hush the matter up. Kilkenny-born Murphy wrote in the *Sunday Independent* that one of the raiders had been killed and the inquest held. The Government admitted the facts the following day, though it took the RUC a further five days to identify the dead man.

The world exclusive on the arms importation should have been the scoop of a distinguished career. It was not published. The editor, Hector Legge, one of the longest serving editors of a national paper, decided not to print the story. He explained the following Sunday that he found himself in conflict as to whether his duty lay to his country or his profession. "I decided not to print the story, holding that the proper place to have the matter raised was in the Dáil," he said.

On May 4th Jack Lynch visited Mount Carmel Hospital in Dublin and asked for the resignation of his then Minister for Justice, Mayo-born Micheal O'Morain. The next day, according to Seamus Brady's book *Arms and the Men* the then opposition leader, Liam Cosgrave visited the Taoiseach, Jack Lynch, and produced an anonymous letter detailing a "plot to import £80,000 worth of arms from the Continent". It named three members of the Cabinet, together with Colonel Heffernon, Director of Army Intelligence, and Captain James Kelly, an army officer working for Army Intelligence. The letter stated that both army officers were "under interrogation in the Bridewell Garda Station."

Later that day the Dublin Spring Show opened at the RDS grounds at Ballsbridge. Neither the Taoiseach nor Neil Blaney, Minister for Agriculture, nor Foreign Affairs Minister Dr. Patrick Hillery showed any visible signs of disunity as they walked through the show grounds to lunch with the RDS committee. The first hint of trouble came at the end of Question Time in the Dáil later that day. With a solemn face, Liam Cosgrave asked the Taoiseach if the resignation from Government of the Minister for Justice, Micheal O' Morain, was "just the tip of the iceberg." Jack Lynch fended off the query with a cryptic remark about being in control of the situation.

Cosgrave, who like his father, W.T. Cosgrave, later became Taoiseach, is believed to have disclosed the arms crisis story the week before to Ned Murphy. After a brief meeting with Fine Gael confidantes, Cosgrave requested a private meeting with Jack Lynch. The two men met in the Taoiseach's office in the Dáil at 8 p.m. It was obvious that Cosgrave knew about the arms importation and was about to "blow the lid" on the whole affair. At 9 p.m. the Taoiseach sent for Neil Blaney and asked for his resignation. Blaney asked for time to consider and said that he would give his answer by 11 o'clock the next day. The Taoiseach replied that "things would happen before then".

Lynch rang Charles Haughey who was still convalescing at home from his riding "accident". Over the phone, Haughey refused to give his resignation. The Taoiseach drafted a short statement for the media for release soon after 11 p.m. But before this was issued, another minister, Kevin Boland, marched into the Taoiseach's office and handed in his resignation. This slightly upset the schedule of events, with the result that the sensational Government press announcement was not made until 2.55 a.m. on May 6th. Lynch announced that Neil Blaney and Charles Haughey had been fired from the Government for alleged involvement in the importation of arms. The reluctant Taoiseach that night revealed himself to be as capable and astute a leader of the Fianna Fáil party as his predecessors Sean Lemass and Eamon de Valera.

The dismissal of Charles Haughey shocked the nation. It was difficult to visualise him as a Republican gunman. As Minister for Finance, he rode to hounds, lived in wealthy comfort in Kinsealy and mixed in the world of financiers, bankers and business leaders. Unlike Neil Blaney, Haughey had never spoken in public on the Northern question. He had remained the figure he had always been to the public - controversial, brilliant and the subject of salacious rumours. Haughey did, however, have a Republican background.

His father, a commandant in the Irish Army, was a County Derry man and joined the army at the instigation of that great Irishman, Michael Collins, who probably did more to free Ireland than any other Irishman. Collins had encouraged a cadre of Northern Republicans to accept commissions with the intention of using them as the nucleus of an armed invasion of the North when the opportunity presented itself after the 1921 Treaty. Former army officers who served with Commandant Haughey recall him as being strongly sympathetic to the Northern minority and outspoken in his views. His premature death left his family in somewhat difficult financial circumstances. (Eamon de Valera, the revered founder of Fianna Fáil, dismissed Haughey in one sentence as "the upstart son of a free state army officer.")

Charles Haughey's mother, a member of the McWilliams family from Maghera, County Derry, was a sturdy Republican and had a strong influence on her son. Charlie spent his summer holidays as a boy with his mother's people in Maghera and came into personal contact with the Northern conflict.

A marathon debate in the Dáil on the arms allegations began on Friday, May 8th and continued for thirty-seven and a half hours, until late on Saturday night May 9th. From the Taoiseach's point of view, it was the next effective step in consolidating his leadership. He already had the support of his own Deputies and the Dáil debate gave him the majority support of parliament. Equally important, he was able to make his first public explanation of his reasons for sacking two Ministers and to present the case against them.

Blaney spoke in the debate and Haughey issued a statement from his home. But neither could offer a defence, partly because they had not broken with the Fianna Fáil party and had to keep to the party political line. There was also a danger of incriminating others if charges should follow.

Charles Haughey issued his denial in a statement from his solicitors. He said: "I regret that on medical advice I cannot make a personal statement to Dáil Eireann concerning the termination of my office as a member of the Government.

"Since becoming a Minister, I have endeavoured to the best of my ability to serve my country, Dáil Eireann and the Government. I have never at any time acted in breach of the trust reposed in me, and I regret that I am now compelled to refer to the circumstances that brought an end to my membership of the Government.

"The Taoiseach informed the Dáil that he requested my resignation on the grounds that he was convinced that not even the slightest suspicion should attach to any member of the Government. I fully subscribe to that view. So far as I have been able to gather, the Taoiseach received information of a nature, which, in his opinion, cast some suspicions on me. I have not had the opportunity to examine or test such information or the quality of its source or sources.

"In the meantime, however, I now categorically state that at no time have I taken part in any illegal importation or attempted importation of arms into this country."

The clear inference in Haughey's statement was that any attempted importation of arms was made with the authority of the Minister for Defence, the late Jim Gibbons, and therefore legal.

Neil Blaney spoke on the opening day of the Dáil debate. With characteristic bluntness, the Donegal deputy told the Dáil: "I want to say I have run no guns; I have procured no guns; I have paid for no guns and I have not provided any money to pay for guns. Anyone who says otherwise is not telling the truth." He attacked those spreading innuendoes and trying to link his name with illegal organisations and "that lousy outfit, Saor Eire." He defended his own and Haughey's brothers, who had been accused by Liam Cosgrave (under privilege of parliament) of gunrunning. He went into his family background and told how he was born while his father was a Free State prisoner under sentence of death, how he had been pulled out of his cot as an infant by Special Branch detectives searching his family home for arms. As a boy he had fought what he termed "Blueshirt bullies".

Several opposition deputies criticised his speech as being "filled with hate". An exception was the Fine Gael deputy for Donegal, Paddy Harte, who had a word of charity for the dismissed Ministers. He praised their "sincerity and dedication".

Opposition leader Liam Cosgrave claimed that but for his action in going to the Taoiseach the whole affair would have been concealed from the public. The people, he asserted, had "been betrayed with their own money." He said that Ireland could thank God for the second time in fifty years that "they had the Fine Gael party to maintain and assert the people's rights." He told the House that he and his party had prevented a civil war of a religious character.

Taoiseach Jack Lynch gave his explanation of how information had come to him from the Special Branch and the Department of Justice, how he had conducted his own investigation. The two Ministers concerned had denied involvement in the plot as alleged, but he could not allow the finger of suspicion to point at any member of the Government. He paid tribute to the men he had dismissed. They were "able and brilliant" and it was "a sad day that our ministerial paths had to part." They had "strong family traditions of service to the country in the fight for freedom" which his family had not. But Jack Lynch insisted that as Taoiseach his "primary duty was to the country" and he "did not shirk it."

He ended by accusing the Opposition of irresponsibility in trying to convince the country that a national emergency was on hand, with bogus threats of a coup d'etat or a civil war. They were "playing with lives" because of the tense situation in the North of Ireland and they had demonstrated clearly that they could offer no responsible alternative to a Fianna Fáil Government.

Winding up the debate for the opposition, Dr. Garret Fitzgerald (later to become Taoiseach) told the country what was behind the dismissals. He said that both Blaney and Haughey were acting in close association with the IRA; the dismissed Minister for Justice, Micheal O Morain, was actively assisting them in importing arms; while Jim Gibbons had been an agent provocateur who had betrayed all three to the Taoiseach. Captain James Kelly, described as the "fall guy" had been used by Gibbons to bring about the downfall of the three Ministers.

He described Blaney as a second Paisley - ruthless, sinister and ambitious. Haughey was a man of great ability, but arrogant and unscrupulous, while Boland was sincere, but misguided and irresponsible. When the Dáil debate concluded, Haughey was forced to swallow his pride and vote confidence in his Taoiseach who had sacked him, and Jack Lynch got approval for his new Ministers by 73 votes to 66.

At the subsequent trial over the arms affair Mr. Justice Henchy spelled out the blunt truth of what had transpired during evidence. Somebody was lying, he said. "Either Charles Haughey or Jim Gibbons was a liar and either Charles Haughey or Peter Berry was a liar." Peter Berry was the Secretary of the Department of Justice. The jury finally retired at 4.50 p.m. on the fourteenth day of the second trial. Within fifty minutes they returned with a verdict of not guilty against all the accused. A crowd of some 500 people, gathered in the wide foyer of the Four Courts, went wild as news of the verdict reached them. In the courthouse, people cheered and stood on seats. Some of the accused rushed to shake hands with jurors. Charles Haughey believed at the time (and many shared his view) that British intelligence could have been responsible for leaking the story about the arms crisis.

The political crisis in Dublin marked the moment in Northern Ireland where the Republic decided to put its own safety first and ceased to try to exercise a restraining influence over militant republicanism in the North of Ireland. Memory of the Arms Crisis tied the hands of successive governments who might otherwise have grappled more directly with violence.

During the Dáil debate after the sacking of the ministers, Brian Lenihan, himself a Minister in the Lynch Government, asked permission from Fianna Fáil Whip Michael Carty for a "pair" with the opposition. That in effect meant that the opposition would withdraw one of their members if there was a vote. Brian Lenihan told Carty that he wanted to visit his friend, Charles Haughey, who was still recovering from his accident. Carty agreed to the request. Listening to the conversation in the room was the late Erskine Childers, who later became an outstanding President. Childers, who was Tanaiste (Deputy Prime Minister) in the Lynch Government, waited until Lenihan left the room then told Carty that as far as he was concerned, Haughey was a traitor and it was "disgraceful" that a member of the Cabinet (Lenihan) should be visiting a person who was "guilty of treason". In any other country, said Childers, Haughey would have been tried for his crime.

Kevin Boland, a Minister who resigned in protest over the sacking of Haughey and Boland, spoke about the affair in 1998, during a special interview on the popular Vincent Browne Radio Programme. He told Browne that he was aware of the arms importation before the crisis erupted. Charlie Haughey came to his office to tell him about the shipment of arms that was going to be acquired.

Vincent Browne – I must put to you Kevin that Charles Haughey said under oath during the course of the arms trial that he knew nothing about it. You are saying now that he not only knew about it at the time but he told you about it in advance?

Kevin Boland – That's right. Yes.

Browne – What did you say to him when he told you this?

Boland – I said I hope you have a reliable chain of authority who will ensure that these weapons will only be used when there is no alternative to going in and helping the Civil Rights people who were being beaten up in the Six Counties at the time.

Browne – What did you feel about him saying ... subsequently, when he denied in the course of the Arms Crisis, when he denied it under oath in the High Court that he knew anything about this? You knew this to be untrue. You also knew that his denial jeopardised the defence offered by his co-accused – namely John Kelly, Captain Jim Kelly and Albert Luykz. Did you not feel some obligation to go and say "look it, this isn't true"?

Boland – Well, I didn't do it anyway.

Browne – Kevin, the Fianna Fáil party was divided down the middle between the factions believing Jim Gibbons and the factions believing Charles Haughey. You were perceived as being one of Haughey's allies and you are saying that Gibbons was essentially telling the truth as he knew it and Haughey was not doing so.

Boland – Well, he (Haughey) was telling a certain amount of the truth, but when he denied that he was involved in it, then he was not telling the truth.

Later, Boland revealed that he tried to get Charles Haughey to join his new party, Aontacht Eireann.

Haughey said he was staying where he was because "that's the place to be if you want to stick a knife in a man's back. You want to be close to him."

Browne – Who was he referring to?

Boland – He was thinking of (Jack) Lynch of course.

—oOo—

In May 1970 rumours circulated throughout the country that

Haughey's fall from a horse was not a genuine one. So concerned was Mr. Haughey about these rumours that he requested his solicitor and long time friend, the late Pat O'Connor, to call a special press conference at his residence in Kinsealy, the purpose of which was to "allay rumours that Mr. Haughey had been beaten up." Before the conference, Mr. Haughey, dressed in a blue blazer, casual shirt and white tennis shoes, made a brief appearance around the house. He looked pale but told reporters he was "picking up" after his horrific injuries. He declined to pose for photographs.

Mr. O'Connor then read a statement from one of Mr. Haughey's medical advisors. It said the former Minister suffered a fractured skull, torn right ear-drum, broken right collar bone and a fracture of the tip of one of the bones in his back. He had severe concussion. The doctor's statement said that Mr. Haughey was making satisfactory progress. But he still suffered from post concussion headache and vertigo. It would be several weeks before he could make a full recovery.

A witness told newsmen she believed Mr. Haughey was dead after he had fallen from his horse. The girl gave a graphic, detailed and comprehensive account of what happened.

She said Mr. Haughey had gone riding on his horse Marshall at 8 a.m. on Budget Day. He returned to the yard at 8.30 a.m. "At the stable door he reached up to catch an overhead drain pipe to lift himself off. The horse sprang forward and the pipe cracked and broke under the strain of Mr. Haughey's grip. He came crashing to the ground backward between the animal and the stable door.

"He was unconscious. There was blood pouring from his ear and mouth. I thought he was dead. I ran to the other yard to get help."

Mr. Haughey was on the ground for about 10 minutes and unconscious for about five, according to the witness. She added: "He got up, but was unsteady on his feet and with other members of staff I helped him as he staggered across the yard. He did not know where he was and kept asking what had happened."

The conference, however, came to an abrupt end a couple of minutes later when an *Evening Press* reporter asked some probing questions. He queried whether or not Mr. Haughey had been seen in a local hotel the evening before the accident. Sensing problems, Pat O'Connor brought the conference to an end.

The following day, an *Evening Herald* reporter rang the Taoiseach's wife, Maureen Haughey, to speak to her about the accident. He asked for details about the drainpipe and the distance it was from the ground. That story, apparently, completely took her by surprise. Her brief reply: "Is that what they are saying; is that what they told you?" she said.

In his memoirs, Peter Berry the former Secretary of the Department of Justice wrote about the incident. He stated that on Budget Day the Garda Commissioner telephoned him to say that the Minister for Finance, Mr. Haughey, had an accident in a fall from a horse and that he was in the Mater Nursing Home.

Berry wrote: "I informed the Taoiseach who had already heard it from another source. Later, the Commissioner phoned me again to say that a strange rumour was circulating in North County Dublin that Mr. Haughey's accident occurred on a licensed premises on the previous night. We discussed the matter and I said that I had better tell the Taoiseach that, too, making it clear that this was not police business and that unless he otherwise directed, the Commissioner would not have any official enquiries made.

"When I informed the Taoiseach of the rumour, as reported by the Commissioner, he said: 'Oh no, not that, too'. And he went on to agree that there should be no police enquiries; he was emphatic on that. I conveyed the Taoiseach's view to the Commissioner.

"Within a couple of days there were all sorts of rumours in golf clubs, in political circles, etc as to how the accident occurred with various husbands, fathers, brothers or lovers having struck the blow in any one of dozens of pubs around Dublin. In short, the accident served a Rabeiaisian purpose without anybody really believing that it was other than a fall from a horse.

"One anecdote: 'Did you hear the real story: Charlie did not fall off the horse, he fell off a filly'. There was nothing much to it, the rumour was partly in affection for a public figure who was attractive to women.

"But when a new Minister, Des O'Malley, was appointed in

May (to succeed Micheal O'Morain), he questioned me as to the rumours and I told him of the Taoiseach's view that there should be no enquiry and that I had so informed the Commissioner. "The Minister said: 'I order you to tell me of any information which you were given and I order you to tell the Commissioner that. I want to know any information that has come to the notice of the local Gardaí.' I told the Minister one of the most far fetched yarns that had come to my ears (which no man in his senses would believe) and I conveyed what he had said to the Commissioner who replied, dryly, that if the Minister were to give him an order in writing he would consider it. That ended that."

Despite the then Taoiseach's view that there should be no investigation, there was one. The local Garda sergeant prepared a file. He needed guidance. So he contacted his superiors. The "chalice" was eventually passed to Peter Berry, Secretary of the Department of Justice. And in compliance with the orders of his Minister, he passed on the information to the newly appointed Minister for Justice, Des O'Malley. O'Malley was asked what should be done. The young Minister thought briefly about the request. He considered the fact that Charles Haughey was now a broken man, sacked from the Government and beginning his political wilderness. "Nothing," he said to Peter Berry, Mr. Haughey has suffered enough. The tough-talking, no-nonsense Limerick solicitor, was later to become Charles Haughey's political bete noire for almost thirty years.

23

FUN AND GAMES
IN HIGH PLACES

To friends and colleagues, Mr. Haughey recalled some of the funniest moments of his career. One of the most hilarious was the wine-changing incident on his island home at Inishvickillane in County Kerry.

Workmen were finishing off the stone-faced bungalow on the island when CJ arrived for a brief holiday. He brought with him a couple of cases of red vintage wine and left them at the bungalow.

The workmen were a thirsty lot and usually brought five or six barrels of Guinness with them. The leader of the group, Dan Brick was due to sail for the mainland one week-end when the weather broke and a storm raged for a couple of days. In the house they spotted the wine and not realising it was vintage, carefully removed the corks and drank the lot. When the weather finally cleared they went to the mainland and bought wine in Garvey's Off Licence in Dingle at £1.50 a bottle. Back on the island they filled the empty bottles and put back the original corks. No problem, as far as they were concerned – they had made good the borrowed wine.

The following summer CJ returned to the island with a VIP whom he was trying to impress. Proudly, he showed him his "vintage" wine and with the room at the right temperature uncorked a bottle. He asked his guest to sample it first. The VIP did not want to insult his host, so he said it was "perfect". Then CJ had a sip, and immediately spat it out. It tasted like vinegar.

He opened a couple more bottles and they were no better. He was mystified and it was a year before he found out what happened. He met Dan Brick on the island and Dan told him how they had run out of Guinness in a storm the previous year, and had to resort to drinking wine. Seeing the look of shock in CJs face and sensing that there was something seriously wrong Dan added: "But we replaced it all." CJs reaction? According to close friends, he nearly fell off his chair ... laughing!

—-oOo—-

His sense of humour was demonstrated at a private meeting with travel journalist, Gerry O Hare. Gerry, who now publishes a glossy magazine, *Travel Extra* was a leading member of the Provisional IRA in the early 70s and spent some time in Portlaoise prison. Later neighbours in Kinsealy, the Taoiseach and O'Hare met at a function. The controversy raging at the time was a new drainage pipeline being installed in Mr. Haughey's estate and in Kinsealy village. O'Hare casually remarked to Haughey: "I had a terrible messy morning. They were out digging up my garden."

Quick as a blink, CJ quipped: "Did they find anything?"

—-oOo—-

And there is a story told about an amusing meeting in a Swords Co. Dublin pub with the former, controversial Minister for Foreign Affairs, Ray Burke, now the subject of a planning inquiry. On the wall of the pub were pictures of some of famous actors, including Edward G. Robinson, who mostly played the role of a gangster. Pointing to the picture of Edward G, CJ quipped to his former Minister: "I see you are remembered here."

Ray had a classic rejoinder: "But you are around the corner, Taoiseach."

Mr. Haughey walked to the next lounge to see a picture of the 1920s Chicago mobster - Al Capone!

—-oOo—-

Senator Don Lydon, a psychologist in St. John of God's Stillorgan, Dublin, decided to offer some useful advice to Mr. Haughey as to why the party had lost a recent election. As he pinpointed some obvious mistakes, Haughey interrupted him with a growl: "Wait a minute; I don't want a fucking shrink to tell me why we lost the election. I want someone to tell me how we can win the next one. Fuck off out of here."

The Fianna Fáil leader's office is neatly panelled in pine. Lydon had difficulty finding the door. CJ looked up from his desk to find the Senator still there. "Are ye still here?" he barked.

"I can't find the door," came the reply.

"Well, jump out the fucking window, so," came the reply.

—-oOo—-

One of the many legacies of Mr. Haughey is the impressive Government Buildings, which were completely refurbished when he was in office. The centerpiece of the buildings is a square at the front in the middle of which is situated a splendid fountain. When lit up at night, it is an impressive sight. During construction, mandarins in the Department of Finance were worried that the project was over running in expenditure. A pruning exercise was suggested by one official, whose memorandum eventually landed on the desk of Mr. Haughey. One proposal was to remove the fountain from the project.

The Taoiseach examined the document in the presence of his secretary, then gave him decisive instructions: "Shred them!"

Without raising his head he added: "And the official who made these suggestions ...? "

"Yes?" queried the secretary.

"You can fucking shred him too!"

—-oOo—-

The former Taoiseach was involved in hilarious incidents with some of the world's top leaders. Like the former British Prime Minister, Margaret Thatcher.

His attention to detail was legendary. For the European Summit in Dublin in 1990 he despatched his head of protocol at

Dublin Castle, Vincent Cullen, to Brussels to find out how the Belgians were handling "yer wan", as he called her.

The blunt message CJ gave Vincent Cullen was: "I want ours to be fucking better! Keep your eyes open and have a look around and go up and check what 'that wan' is getting." Vincent peered into her bedroom, checked out her bathroom and discovered that she had especially installed all sorts of exotic perfumes, soaps, towels and toiletries. Six months later, it was Ireland's turn to host the European summit at Dublin Castle. CJ met Vincent Cullen and said: "I hope you will have the place looking well for "yer wan" to-morrow." He instructed him to put everything Irish in the room. Cullen bought all his toiletries in Arnott's, the big Dublin department store. As usual, CJ inspected all the rooms at Dublin Castle before the Prime Ministers arrived. He was accompanied by his Press Secretary, P.J. Mara, who immediately sampled the Thatcher bed and joked irreverently: "This will do the oul bitch." CJ peeped into the bathroom and shouted at Vincent Cullen: "This is a bit much!" CJ was looking at the well-known Irish perfume Man of Aran, by *Vincent!* Mrs. Thatcher was obviously pleased with the Irish perfumes and toiletries. When staff arrived to clean up the rooms after the summit was over, the toiletries were all cleared from her bathroom.

Earlier, the Taoiseach was informed by one of his officials that the Thatcher helicopter was approaching Dublin Castle. A couple of moments later, the same official announced "She has arrived now, Taoiseach." Mr. Haughey walked out on the bridge to meet her. The wind from the rotor blades blew his hair all over the place. CJ quickly got back inside the door, wet his fingers and with difficulty managed to pat his hair down. An official said to the Taoiseach: "She is on the bottom step now." CJ stepped out again and the wind stood his hair up again. He turned to his bemused officials and said: "Ah fuck it, let her come to me." When she greeted the Taoiseach moments later, Mrs. Thatcher had to say hello with one hand holding down her hair.

Just two days after the EC summit, another VIP arrived – South African President Nelson Mandela, only recently released from prison and in Ireland to be made a Freeman of Dublin. In the motorcade through Dublin, the South African hero encountered some typical Dublin wit. The chant for the great

Irish soccer hero, Paul McGrath had been: "Ooh ah, Paul McGrath". As Nelson Mandela motored through Dublin, the chant changed: "Ooh ah, Paul McGrath's Da!" Tired and a little sick, Mandela requested a bed on his arrival at Dublin Castle. The problem was that all the beds had been removed. The only one left was in the Thatcher room.

A couple of hours later, CJ arrived and asked Vincent Cullen: "Where is he Vincent?" Cullen replied: "He is resting."

Haughey pursued: "Where did you put him?" Cullen did not want to say "Maggie's room", so he told his Taoiseach embarrassingly "The room at the end of the corridor." CJ immediately spotted Cullen's embarrassment and asked: "Is that where 'yer wan' was last night?"

"Yes," came the admission.

"Not the fucking same bed?"

Cullen nodded: "Yes."

The Taoiseach closed his eyes and quipped: "Jesus don't let the press get a hold of that!"

—oOo—

There were some amusing incidents involving the late French President, Francois Mitterand, a close friend who enjoyed Mr. Haughey's hospitality on his island home at Inishvickillane in County Kerry.

During the EC Summit, CJ always gave preferential treatment to the French President. As far as he was concerned Mitterand wore two hats. He was the President of France and effectively the Prime Minister. Though Mrs. Thatcher, as the only female Prime Minister, wanted to be received last, Mr. Haughey insisted on giving that honour to his friend, Francois.

Walking up the corridor of Dublin Castle, Mr. Haughey was proudly showing off the imposing paintings of some of the previous occupants. Mitterand stopped and peered at a painting of Lord Hardwick, the English Viceroy. "Ah", he said, "he is very like you." Mr. Haughey was not amused to be told that he was the spitting image of a hated English Viceroy.

Mitterand particularly admired the statue of Louis 14th in Dublin Castle, and therein lies an amusing tale. Four years after the Summit, Mitterand was in Ireland for a State visit. He was scheduled to attend a dinner at the splendidly decorated Royal Hospital in Kilmainham, Dublin. Officials from the Taoiseach's department insisted on a French ambience for the visit. And one of the "bright" officials thought it would be a good idea to haul the Louis the 14th statue from Dublin Castle to Kilmainham. They had great difficulty with it. They got a crane, delicately pulled it out through a window that had to be removed, and a big truck then hauled it from Dublin Castle to Kilmainham. They placed it in the front hall of the Royal Hospital. The French President arrived and was greeted at the entrance by the Taoiseach. Once inside the door, he spotted the statue and joked to the embarrassed Taoiseach: "Ah, I see you have moved Louis from the Castle."

CJs comment to his staff later: "Jaysus that was some fucking bright idea!"

—-oOo—

While Minister for Health in 1979, Haughey brought in a controversial Family Planning Bill that regularised Family Planning Centres so that they could lawfully provide condoms throughout the country. Journalist Kevin Moore, health correspondent of the *Irish Independent,* broke the story about the Haughey Bill. Chatting with the Minister at his office in the Custom House, Moore remarked that it was highly unlikely that the Irish Medical Association would agree to their doctors prescribing condoms for patients.

Haughey's tongue in cheek reply: "Listen Kevin, those fuckers will do anything for money!"

—-oOo—

One of the most amusing stories came from his "sessions" with his old pals, the late Brian Lenihan and the late colourful Minister for Education, Donogh O'Malley. The three of them, in their drinking days, were a formidable trio – affectionately known as "The Three Musketeers."

The three Ministers had time on their hands on a quiet

morning in the Dáil. They decided to treat themselves to lunch in the Russell Hotel, just off St. Stephen's Green in the city centre. Outside the hotel was a bearded buskar in tattered clothes, playing the accordion. The buskar, reasonably talented, was accompanied by his scruffy-haired mongrel dog. The three Ministers decided to treat the buskar and his dog to a lunch. To the annoyance of the management and staff, the musician warmly entertained the three Ministers. All four enjoyed themselves – particularly the lavish meal.

A couple of weeks later, O'Malley, then the Health Minister, was shocked when he received the bill. He immediately rang the manager to query it. "We could not have eaten that amount of food," he protested. "There were only the three of us and the musician.

" Back came the reply from the manager. "What about the dog. He cleared all the deserts on the trolly!"

24

NEW ALLEGATIONS BEFORE TRIBUNAL

New revelations on bankrolling former Taoiseach, Charles Haughey are contained in a recent submission to the Moriarty Tribunal, as investigations continue into payments made to him.

The document submitted to the Moriarty Tribunal does not state whether or not the "substantial" financial contribution from the Irish company was personal to Mr. Haughey or for the Fianna Fáil party.

When the Moriarty Tribunal opened its public hearings in January 1999, the secret financing of Charles Haughey's lavish lifestyle was laid bare. The ex-Taoiseach sustained his champagne lifestyle through a string of shadowy financial arrangements, including £1.3m for supermarket magnate, Ben Dunne. It was disclosed by Counsel for the Tribunal that the country's biggest bank, Allied Irish, was offered a £10m cheap loan facility as part of an arrangement to write off money owed by Haughey. The loan was to come from a Middle East bank in 1979 in return for writing off half of Mr. Haughey's £1.1m debt. The £10m deposit would have provided AIB with cheap money to loan to customers at favourable interest rates. Mr. Haughey's accountant Des Traynor appears to have sought a commission, worth up to £600,000 for Mr. Haughey for arranging the bond. But AIB rejected the proposal.

The Tribunal's first day of public hearings at Dublin Castle also heard of various other plans to repay part of Mr. Haughey's loans and write off debts, including a series of payments from

Dunnes Stores between 1987 and 1992 amounting to more than £803,000. Details of negotiations between AIB bank executives and Mr. Haughey's financial adviser, Des Traynor, since deceased, indicated that the former Fianna Fáil leader had pressing financial problems when he took over from Jack Lynch in December 1979. Three payments from the Guinness & Mahon Bank in 1980 cut Mr. Haughey's debts at AIB to £110,000 after the bank wrote off one quarter as a "commercially justified settlement". And it was revealed to the Tribunal that Mr. Haughey never paid the remaining £110,000 debit balance in his account at AIB.

Details were also given of the £803,900 transferred from Dunnes Stores to Mr. Haughey's benefit and of £100,000 given to Celtic Helicopters, of which Ciaran Haughey, Mr. Haughey's son, is the major shareholder.

In the King George Hall at Dublin Castle, with its magnificent antique chandeliers, Counsel for the Tribunal, Mr. John Coughlan, SC, used large screens on the wall to chart various cheque payments. He described negotiations between Mr. Haughey and Des Traynor with AIB to reduce his debts. Proposals included selling land at Baldoyle. Another proposal was that some of the 248 acres of land surrounding Haughey's mansion at Abbeyville would be sold or transferred to property developer, Patrick Gallagher.

On the 27th day of the inquiry, the Tribunal heard that a Saudi Arabian diplomat passed on a £50,000 payment, through former minister Dr. John O'Connell to buy a racehorse from Charles Haughey in 1985.

The Tribunal was also told about lodgements of more than £1.5m to Mr. Haughey's bank accounts over an eight-year period.

The inquiry heard that Mr. Haughey had four operating accounts in the Guinness and Mahon Bank from 1979, but it appeared he did not lodge the proceeds of his salary cheques to any of his bank accounts.

Tribunal counsel Jerry Healy said lodgements to these accounts were "very significant" and the relative size of the total of the sums lodged to these accounts and the amounts of individual lodgements could be judged when it was borne in mind that in 1979 a TD was paid an annual salary of £9,590.

The Tribunal was also told that Mr. Haughey has refused to give a waiver granting the Moriarty Tribunal access to records of his dealings with Ansbacher Bank on the Cayman Islands.

Mr. Haughey has given the Tribunal access to his Irish bank accounts – although the Tribunal would have been able to gain access anyway. The same is not true for the secretive Cayman Islands.

It was disclosed to the Tribunal that in 1983 Mr. Haughey got a £400,000 loan from Ansbacher (Cayman) Ltd., then called Guinness Mahon Cayman Trust and a subsidiary of Guinness & Mahon Bank (G&M) Dublin. At the time Mr. Haughey had a number of accounts in his name with the Dublin bank but the £400,000 was not lodged to any of them. The Tribunal has not yet been able to identify where it went.

In his subsequent application to the Central Bank to take out this loan, Mr. Haughey told the Central Bank that he wanted the funds to develop his Kinsealy stud farm. The application was approved. Six days after the loan application was made, Mr. Haughey was replaced as Taoiseach by Dr. Garret FitzGerald.

At the time a Taoiseach's salary was about £17,000 and a TD's salary was about £10,000. The loan was repaid around 1987 when Mr. Haughey was returning or had returned to power.

The Tribunal also learned that money lodged to one of Haughey's bank accounts came from a loan account in the name of the late hotelier PV Doyle. Mr. Doyle had opened the loan facility in 1983 at Guinness and Mahon Bank because Mr. Haughey was "financially embarrassed". But it eventually became clear that there was no hope of repaying the loan and the Doyle Hotel Group eventually cleared the debt.

25

EPILOGUE

After his last meeting as leader of the Fianna Fáil parliamentary party in 1992, Charles Haughey shook hands with the Chairman, Jim Tunney, a shrewd politician who had presided over many controversial meetings during the previous twelve years.

"I want to say to you, Jim," he volunteered in an emotional voice, "that over the years I never took a penny from the Irish taxpayer".

From our investigations, this statement appears to be correct. Mr. Haughey financed his lavish lifestyle, including the money he spent on the wining and dining of Terry Keane, out of his own personal account. Taxpayers' money was never used.

---oOo---

In a garage in Clontarf, Dublin, an unusual collection of gifts has been gathering dust. The items were put together by Dublin North Central TD, Ivor Callely a Fianna Fáil member of the Dáil for Dublin North Central. In 1997, he suggested that particular items from the collection should be presented to former Fianna Fáil members of the Dáil.

The party leader, Taoiseach Bertie Ahern, agreed to the suggestion but before any action could be taken on the plan, the spotlight was turned on former Taoiseach Charles Haughey, former senior government minister Ray Burke, and the then Euro Commissioner, Padraig Flynn. All three were implicated in allegations about political payments and three separate tribunals headed by Judges McCracken, Flood and Moriarty, were established to delve into these allegations. It was decided for obvious reasons to let the collection gather a little more dust in Clontarf until the hare settled and the tribunals had completed their work, and that turned out to be one of Bertie Ahern's better decisions.

---oOo---

When Jack Lynch was the leader of Fianna Fáil, he signed all party cheques in the presence of the 80-member National Executive, the ruling body, and usually they were presented to him just as meetings were ending. When Charles Haughey became leader of the party in 1979, he ended this particular ceremony. He took the cheques home with him to sign.

---oOo---

Shortly after Haughey controversially returned to the Fianna Fáil front bench in 1975, one of the stalwarts of the party, former Minister for External Affairs, the late Frank Aitken, a close friend of the founder Eamon de Valera, spoke at a national executive meeting of the party. He made it clear that because of Haughey's return he himself had decided not to go forward again at the next general election. At the same time, however, he said he wanted a young politician from Derry to succeed him, a Credit Union activist and Civil Rights campaigner. That man was John Hume, who later became leader of the Northern nationalist party, the SDLP, who went on to a distinguished political career in the European Parliament. And for his untiring efforts to find a just peace in Northern Ireland in 1998 he was jointly awarded the Nobel Peace Prize with Ulster Unionist leader, David Trimble.

---oOo---

In 1975, the former controversial Minister for Defence, the late Jim Gibbons, whose evidence at the Arms Trial totally contradicted that of Charles Haughey, and the late George Colley sought a meeting with the then leader, Jack Lynch. While in opposition, Lynch had brought Haughey back from the political wilderness, and appointed him Health spokesman. Gibbons and Colley demanded to know why Lynch had taken such a decision. The Taoiseach replied only that since he was preaching reconciliation in the North, he had to be seen to be practising it down here.

---oOo---

In 1966 when George Colley, then Minister for Industry and Commerce, was in the United States on a trade mission, the then Taoiseach, Sean Lemass, sent him a telegram stating: "Your return should not be delayed." Lemass was about to announce his resignation and wanted Colley back for the leadership contest in which his son-in-law Charles Haughey was the other candidate. At that time, George Colley's supporters reckoned that the vote against Haughey would be 58 to 22. But because of the divisive nature of the struggle for party leadership, party elders put forward a compromise candidate, Jack Lynch, who eventually defeated Colley by 61 votes to 19.

---oOo---

Since I have mentioned Sean Lemass it is perhaps worth recalling another story involving him and his son-in-law. There is a portrait of him in the Haughey mansion "Abbeyville". Obviously, Charles Haughey had a great affection for his father-in-law. But was it reciprocated?

At a barbecue in Kinsealy in the late sixties, a friend of Haughey's was chatting with the pipe-smoking former Taoiseach in the solitude of the house, away from the drinking and the revelry going on outside in the yard. The friend commented on the superb antiques, including the furniture, paintings and silver in the spacious hallway of the grand house, joking that with the big crowd around the family had better keep a sharp eye on it!

Lemass let his eyes sweep around the walls as he puffed on his pipe. "Aye," he said. "But where is it all coming from?"

When Haughey finally succeeded Lynch as Taoiseach in 1979, Colley agreed to serve in cabinet on one condition. He wanted a veto over the selection of the Minister for Defence and Justice. Extraordinarily this demand was made to Haughey during a meeting at the home of Senator Eoin Ryan, the same Senator Ryan who resigned from the Fianna Fáil Finance Committee as soon as Haughey took over. At that time, most of the old guard in Fianna Fáil and current Cabinet members did not want to serve under Haughey. Colley had to persuade them to serve. Haughey mentioned that he was grateful to his former classmate for the loyalty he had shown to him. But Colley had reservations about Haughey, and gave only conditional support to him. For example, he made it quite clear to him that because of the way he had undermined former leader Jack Lynch, he would support him as Taoiseach but not as leader of Fianna Fáil. This sent a clear signal to the Fianna Fáil organisation throughout the country that the new Taoiseach was suspect and was not to be trusted.

When forming a Government, Haughey had to re-appoint a substantial number of the outgoing Lynch cabinet. But he surprised the organisation by increasing the number of parliamentary secretaries from ten to fifteen. He used these junior appointments as watchdogs to maintain control and put his own stamp on the party.

---oOo---

A young, attractive Fine Gael Senator was so concerned about the new Family Planning legislation being enacted in 1977 that she sought a personal meeting with the new Minister for Health, Charles Haughey. When she arrived for the meeting, he dismissed his official from his office in the Custom House. When the lady began to outline her anxieties about the impending legislation, he interrupted her to say: "I don't think the billings method would suit you or I". A few years later when the Senator became a TD and Charles Haughey became Taoiseach, he walked behind her in the Dáil gallery during a vote and began to playfully grope her. The young TD, though in awe of the Taoiseach, quickly put him in his place.

Charlie Haughey's wife Maureen and members of the family were deeply hurt by the revelations of the Keane – Haughey romance in the Dermot Morgan satirical RTE show Scrap Saturday. One of Mr. Haughey's sons approached journalist Sam Smyth and asked him if he could do something about it. Sam suggested that they should speak to *Sunday Independent* diarist, Terry Keane, who was constantly writing about the romance. Representations were later made to RTE without success.

The Keane Edge column in the *Sunday Independent* also brought distress to the Haughey household. Former Miss Ireland, Siobhan Mc Clafferty and her sister, Jacqui, who married Conor Haughey, were strolling the Abbeyville grounds one Sunday morning. They walked into the kitchen to find the *Sunday Independent* and the *Keane Edge* column spread out on the table ...

Obviously distressed sitting on a chair was Maureen Haughey. She was sobbing.

—-oOo—-

The captain of the Celtic Mist a 60-foot motor sailer that has provided immense pleasure for Charlie Haughey, his family and his mistress, Terry Keane, had been employed on a permanent basis– until recently. He received a call from Mr. Haughey saying that he could not justify retaining him on salary given the revelations in the various tribunals.

Mr. Haughey told him that he would have to regretfully terminate his employment. The experienced captain, who had worked for Mr. Haughey for a long time, has since found other employment.

—-oOo—-

At a Fianna Fáil fund raiser in the Plaza Hotel in New York in 1997, attended by the Taoiseach, Bertie Ahern, Irish passports were freely sought by the well-heeled American businessmen.

One Texas banker approached a table which was hosted by Environment Minister, Noel Dempsey. He offered an open cheque to the Minister in return for an Irish passport.

In polite terms, the Meath politician told him to get lost.

The big question is how much, if anything, did Maureen Haughey know about the affair between her husband and Terry Keane. It is known that she did receive an anonymous letter more than a decade ago and was worried enough about the contents to consult the late Padraig O hAnrachain, close friend and advisor to her husband.

She showed him the letter and he advised her to disregard it.

"Never take any notice of anonymous letters," he assured her. It was only malicious gossip.

—oOo—

Returning from a presentation of the Irish business awards at RTE, Charles Haughey, then Taoiseach, phoned Terry Keane on his mobile car phone – not knowing that an electronics expert was listening on the frequency!

The expert was testing cellular interception equipment when he heard the Taoiseach's rasping voice talking to a posh English female. He later recognised the speaker as Terry Keane.

Charlie told Terry he was with Max (his driver) and was a bit "pissed" having come from the RTE hospitality suite. He assured her he was "on his way" to the hotel suite which they had booked.

The couple were laughing and giggling and Terry was heard to say that the flowers were "fine" but she joked that there were no chocolates.

Charlie asked her how he looked on television. She replied: "You looked fine – as you always do".

The conversation became muffled then. But Terry was heard to say that anyone would look good in that drab Irish company.

—oOo—

A dramatic meeting of the Fianna Fáil parliamentary party in 1981 gave an insight into Haughey's duplicity in respect of the Arms Crisis. An article in "Magill" magazine was extremely critical of the role played by him in the importation of arms. The then leader of the opposition, Dr. Garret FitzGerald, put down a motion in the Dáil, condemning the role of Charles Haughey, who was then Taoiseach.

Haughey told a tense party meeting that there would only be one speaker from Fianna Fáil in the subsequent Dáil debate and that was the then Minister for Justice, Gerry Collins.

Former Taoiseach, Jack Lynch, who was still a member of the parliamentary party at the time, rose to say that since his name was mentioned in the "Magill" article he intended to speak. He was followed by the former Minister for Defence, the late Jim Gibbons, a central figure in the arms crisis. Gibbons told his colleagues that he also intended to speak.

There was an eerie silence. Eventually a newly elected Senator from Galway, Professor Jim Doolan, brother-in-law of Mr. Haughey's great political rival, George Colley, stood up. He told a hushed meeting that since the issue raised by Dr. FitzGerald touched on the integrity of the leader of Fianna Fáil – and by implication the Fianna Fáil party – he was surprised that the leader was not going to address the issue.

While Doolan was on his feet posing the question, a quorum bell rang in the Dáil. The meeting came to an abrupt end and the matter had to be dropped. At the end of the meeting, Professor Doolan walked up from the back of the hall to the top table, where Charles Haughey was standing. Haughey glared at his former accountancy colleague – Doolan qualified as an accountant at the Haughey-Boland accountancy firm – and was heard to say in an angry tone that he had been watching him and did not like what he was seeing. He told the U.C.G. Professor of Business Studies that he was "on a slippery slope" and had better watch his step. Doolan replied: "That is a matter of opinion."

Professor Doolan, who was a Fianna Fáil candidate in the 1979 European election, stood for the Senate on five subsequent occasions. Word percolated from Haughey's aides that he was not to be supported. Professor Doolan never won a Seanad or European election seat while Haughey remained leader, but he did continue to speak out about "scandals" and the "autocratic" leadership of Haughey during his twelve years at the helm.

---oOo---

Back in Dublin after an important meeting in Washington, Tanaiste and Foreign Affairs Minister, Brian Lenihan could not contain himself. In a Dublin pub early in the morning, he disclosed to a close friend one of the most bizzare tales of the entire Haughey era.

At the time – early in 1980 – Ireland was heavily in debt and the International Fund had made overtones to the Government to take corrective measures. The new Taoiseach, Charles Haughey, in a celebrated television broadcast, had told the nation that we were living beyond our means and urged us to tighten our belts.

This was the time when the whole international political scene had been thrown into turmoil by the invasion of Afghanistan by the Russians, and the Americans were worried that this was the beginning of a new push by the Soviets to extend their sphere of influence around the world.

In the pub Lenihan told his friend that officials in the Washington administration had come up with a solution to our financial problems. They would clear the debt – provided we would agree to an unusual quid pro quo. Swearing his friend to secrecy, he revealed that the Americans wanted the Irish Government to provide a suitable site to house a nuclear arsenal in Ireland. They suggested that an ideal location was a hydroelectric power station at a place called Turlough Hill in County Wicklow, about 40 miles from Dublin. The national Electricity Service Board had excavated a huge area of rock under the mountain and ran a shaft up the centre to enable turbines to be driven by water tumbling from the mountaintop.

In order to allay the fears of workers at Turlough Hill, the Americans proposed that the Irish Government would purchase the site. It was proposed to install the nuclear arsenal beside the generators – under the mountain.

Brian Lenihan began his conversation with his friend: "You will not believe what is on the cards for Turlough Hill. Certainly, Laragh will never be the same again." In the end the proposal came to naught because the Americans had second thoughts.

---oOo---

In the course of a Dáil debate that followed the attempt to

import arms into the country for the IRA in 1970, the Taoiseach, Jack Lynch, gave an unqualified assurance that no postal warrant in respect of the telephone or correspondence of any member of the Government (or indeed any member of the Dáil or Seanad) had been signed by the Minister for Justice.

Apparently, Mr. Lynch did not know everything that was going on in Government, for a most audacious and sensational phone tap was being orchestrated at that time. A technician working at the Merrion Telephone Exchange situated opposite Government Buildings spotted something unusual one Saturday morning. He found a tap on the main distribution frame. Astonished, he brought the discovery to the attention of his superior, Mr. Jim Dermody. The two men double-checked that it was a genuine tap and discovered that the tap was on the phone of Mr. Lynch. And worse, it was directly linked to the office of the then Minister for Finance, Charles Haughey! Every time the Taoiseach used his phone, his conversation could be heard on the line in Mr. Haughey's office.

The officials immediately terminated the tap, but nobody knew how long this situation had gone on for and though a thorough investigation was carried out to find who was responsible, nobody was ever charged.

---oOo---

Charlie Haughey's wry comment on journalists : "I hate those creeping little shits!" reminds me of my first ever meeting with him in 1981. I was sent by the then Editor of the "Sunday Independent" the late Michael Hand to do a colour story on Haughey who was on the campaign trail in County Kerry. I was picked up at Weston aerodrome near Celbridge, County Kildare and accompanied by one of Charlie's minders, Eoin Patton, was flown to Farranfore Airport in County Kerry. From there I was chauffeur-driven to the quaint town of Kenmare, where the then Taoiseach was electioneering in typical rambunctious style with outgoing Deputy John O' Leary from Killarney and the rising young star from Cahirciveen, the current Minister for Justice, John O'Donoghue.

I was eagerly looking forward to that first meeting. I had read that Charlie was brilliant, erudite, eloquent and had taken first place in Ireland in his primary certificate. He won first class honours in all his subjects at U.C.D., was a chartered accountant and a barrister. He was also an expert on Irish and French history, fluent in both languages and a connoisseur on French wines. In other words, he was gifted in almost everything.

I had hoped that he would share some nuggets of wisdom with me during the trip.

In the back of a helicopter for three hours with his then press secretary, Frank Dunlop, I was seated only a couple of feet from this wonderful man of letters, this walking genius.

During that time, all he said to me was four words: "Close that fucking door"!

Charlie thought I was a member of his security!

---oOo---

In conclusion, I want to make a plea to the Moriarty Tribunal to select a date to conclude their crucial hearings – preferably the end of 1999. But my request is based on a quid pro quo from Charles Haughey.

They can end their hearings speedily – if Mr. Haughey is prepared to fully co-operate and tell the truth, the whole truth and nothing but the truth about all his financial dealings. This would include telling the tribunal what political favours were granted to businessmen who contributed to his lavish lifestyle.

If the Tribunal was brought to a speedy conclusion, the torture would end for the Haugheys, and particularly for his wife Maureen. While the decision rests with Judge Michael Moriarty who heads the Tribunal and ultimately with Charles Haughey, if he is prepared to co-operate, a speedy conclusion would end the agony for the Haughey family and save the taxpayer millions of pounds. (Up to the end of June 1999, the Tribunal has cost £2.6m, with legal fees accounting for a staggering £2m.).

When the Tribunal finally makes a judgement on Mr. Haughey, it will have to take into account the legacy he has left for this country – his contribution to the creation and development of the Celtic Tiger, and indeed of his considerable achievements since he was appointed to his first Ministry at the Department of Justice.